AUTONOMOUS ZONE

CITIZEN HILL

SIMON SAYZ

LG Publishing Partners, LLC

ALSO BY SIMON SAYZ

Want updated information on new releases?
Click HERE to sign up for the Newsletter.

Trapped outside the city in the Autonomous Zone, Citizen Hill finds an unlikely ally in Julian Bless, which brings into question—the enemy of my enemy is my friend, or is he?

Citizen Hill is a genetically enhanced warrior trained since childhood to hunt infected humans and rogue Gollums. When a new faction, Elysium, moves into the Autonomous Zone, declaring ownership, the Therian Federation tasks her with one mission: infiltrate the organization, take the leader, Julian Bless, into custody, and disband the followers. Once on the inside, she discovers a horde of infected humans and Gollums responsible for a shocking series of brutal attacks devastating the Township of New Therian.

These monsters are different, nothing like the

mindless beasts she's fought before—the creatures crave mammalian meat, mainly uninfected humans.

When the Gollums turn on the humans in the Autonomous Zone, slaying whole colonies to eat their flesh, word gets out. The leaders of New Therian, fearing a Gollum invasion, quarantine the city. The act results in a massive lockdown, sealing the New Therian in a dome for fourteen days.

Citizen, forced to turn to the humans of Elysium for survival, finds herself at odds with her programing, her creators, and what it means to be human. Fighting side by side with Julian Bless, she discovers there's more to the virus, the Gollums and Trolls, the Federation Leadership, and her origins.

Several Federation Dignitaries will stop at nothing to erase Citizen Hill and Julian Bless from history and shield the truth of the deadly virus consuming the Autonomous Zone.

For those who dream of a better place. When your soul comes knocking, heed its call to arms.

CONTENTS

SNEAK PEEK: NEW THERIAN
CITY

CITIZEN HILL

"I am Elysium." A cloaked figure at the head of the altar raised a fist. "I. Am. Elysium."

The crimson-colored hood cast a shadow across his face. Patches of pale skin peeked out from beneath the fabric. A scan of his measurements confirmed he matched the height and build of the target.

Found you. She glanced at her surroundings—the crumbling remains of a concrete and steel building taken down five years ago during the first waves of attacks of World War III.

You're definitely not a ghostly aberration.

Those three simplistic words—I am Elysium—

incited a unified chant among the faction occupying the pit of the chamber. Murmured voices, both male and female, rose, producing a combined echo.

Perched on a steel beam on the third floor, over-looking the ceremony, Citizen Hill activated the zoom-in function of the T-581 ocular implant nestled in her left eye. The crosshairs floated together, forming a plus sign, then multiple red dots covered the exposed lower half of the target's profile.

Static, followed by a squelch, squawked in her ear.

"Seventeen percent match." The handler—a feminine voice without a face—grumbled. "Get me more."

Damn, not enough for a raid. She inched out as far as the steel beam allowed.

"A little to the left, you snowball aberration." Her words, only a whisper, escaped her lips like a soft breeze on a frigid autumn morning.

The lines came together once more, and an explosion of red dots filled her vision, at least three times more than the prior scan.

"Hold steady," the handler squawked again, "or you'll lose him."

Refusing to breathe for fear of interrupting the facial recognition, Citizen Hill remained motionless, lids wide open. A Syth-L, short for a synthetic life form, contained major organs like those of a human, but only for show. Like a handful of others, she looked human enough to pass as a fleshy but to do so took up extra space better spent processing necessary intel. Plus, without an emotion chip, she didn't see or feel the need to replicate the simulation of life.

It's not as if Elysium followers care.

"Talk to me," she whispered under her breath, waiting for instructions.

"Sixty-eight percent match, that's enough for now," said the handler. "Stand by for an intel drop." She was new, unknown to Citizen.

Hmm, where's Steel? He's never missed an assignment, not since I went active—and the old-timer's never late.

"Copy that." She considered asking but thought twice about doing so. Handlers and operatives never co-mingled, and they certainly didn't make non-work-related inquiries. "Standing by."

Nothing came. Just static. She refreshed the link.

The white icon in the lower left of her GUI vision spun in a never-ending circular motion. She was losing reception and needed to get to higher ground.

Citizen didn't know how long this ceremony of theirs would last.

Humans have so many bizarre rituals, none of which make sense.

"Sister Citizen." A figure stopped behind her. It was one of the priest elders—the same tall, thin man in the same brown robe, who had greeted her earlier.

Hmm. His footsteps had gone unnoticed to the ear—a most unfortunate turn of events.

She had made contact with the group known as Elysium this morning but had been tracking them for over a week. After surviving the wasteland, Gollums, and infected humans, she had completed the first part of her mission—infiltration. Now, she needed to move on to milestone two—acquire the target.

"Oh, hello." Citizen crawled off her perch and joined him. "I didn't catch your name?"

She kept her voice low, monotone to a degree, to replicate the pitch and rate of the other cult followers.

"I am Master Dunlam, one of Julian Bless' senior supporters." The robed man tucked both of his hands into his long sleeves, like one would a muff, then held them in front of him. "I do hope you will join me with the rest, down below." He cast a suspicious gaze her way.

Citizen needed to get away from Dunlam and the

group to re-establish coms, but that looked like it would have to wait.

"Sure." She replicated a smile with just a peek of teeth for a more natural look.

Master Dunlam motioned for her to lead the way down the winding path of what use to pass for stairs. Static in the connection slowly overtook the channel. The L-5 receiver wasn't cutting it.

I'm definitely upgrading when I return to base. She chewed on which model to try out next.

The L-7 offered new surveillance features. But then again, it came with bugs.

I don't need to fry my circuits as a beta-tester. She sighed, then thought, *the L-6.75 receiver it is.*

"Acknowledge, CH," the handler barked in her ear. Citizen loathed her codename. She hated her serial number too. CH012SYTH-L sounded so lifeless. That's why she gave herself a real name, Citizen Hill.

She sent a busy code of text through the implanted chip connected to her processor so that the priest wouldn't hear.

Her handler switched to messaging, but the connection continued to fade the closer she got to the ground. The broken concrete walls and steel formations made coms harder. That's why she went to the steel beam in the first place. The commlink went dry.

So close, she thought with a sigh.

The lack of response would frustrate HQ, but setbacks come with the territory when in the middle of an infiltration mission.

She and her escort reached the ground level and joined the crowd in the back of the chamber. The group was a little over one hundred by the last head-count. They were all walking in single file across the altar that Bless stood behind.

One at a time, each follower kneeled, bowed his or her head, then placed a hand on the large red stone that sat on the altar. Every last one of them flattened a palm on the stone, remained there silently for a couple of seconds, rose to full height, then walked away. The next person repeated the ritual.

Citizen had no idea what it meant and wasn't going to ask.

"You do not have to take part in the dedication ceremony if you do not understand it." Master Dunlam stood right behind her like the shadow she couldn't shake.

"Okay, thank you," said Citizen, in her best human tone. "I will wait."

After everyone walked by and touched the stone,

Bless finished his address. She knew it was him and didn't need HQ's approval to move in. But this meddling priest was too close to her, though. He had already caught her up on her perch overhead, which made the human suspicious of her, so she must proceed with caution.

Citizen stood next to the figures clothed in dirty rags and ponchos. If she could get lost in the crowd, she could shake free of Master Dunlam, then isolate her target.

2

Octavian Karr

Commander Octavian Karr walked into the control room. Four different handlers sat at an equal number of station ports, each containing control panels. Their eyes remained diligently glued to their screens. Commander Karr brushed his black mustache and made sure his Federation uniform was straight.

His pants, ironed to crisp perfection, were tucked neatly into his tall black leather boots, which he polished to a glossy shine—one he could see his reflection in. He glanced at the other handlers. The wrinkled uniforms, worn belts, and scuffed leather made his skin crawl.

If everyone in the Federation took their jobs as seriously as I do, he thought to himself, *Elysium would die out.*

For this mission with the Syth-L, handler Nev Meechum was assigned. He didn't recognize the name. He hadn't worked with her before, but anyone was better than the do-gooder, Andy Reynolds.

Andy, or codename Steel, had become a liability the last thirty days—one Karr had personally seen to.

When one wants something done right, ya do it yourself. A slight grin crossed his lips. And where Steel was, well, he wouldn't be an issue any longer.

"Handler Meechum," he spoke in an authoritative tone—the one that told his subordinates they were pawns—his to be exact.

A young woman from across the room shot to attention. "Yes, Sir. Handler Meechum, here, Sir."

The other three handlers remained focused on their screens as if not wanting to call attention to themselves.

Karr crossed the floor, closing the gap. "I'm Commander Karr." His boots made loud thuds on the metal floor. "I'm directly in charge of Operation 219. I understand you are now the lead and only handler on this mission."

"That's correct, Sir." Handler Meechum had her

blonde hair pulled into a ponytail. It met regulation. To his surprise, her uniform was spotless. The federation member was disciplined and no rookie, but she seemed a bit too eager for his liking. She was no seasoned veteran either. He would have to keep an eye on her.

"How many solo missions have you successfully completed?" He glanced at the control panel.

"I'm 17 and 0 on solo missions, Sir, and 28 and 11 with team ops."

"And your solo missions, they were all with Syth-Ls, is that correct?"

"That's right, Sir," replied Handler Meechum. "I've been in the handler unit for almost a year now."

"And you've read the file?"

"Yes, Sir. As instructed."

"So, you are aware of the importance of this mission and the level of op sec that's required?"

"Yes, Sir. I've done six Tier One missions before, so I'm familiar with the protocol."

"Have a seat." Karr motioned to the high back stool at her station. "Pull up the operative's chart."

She tapped the flat screen to life, and her hands slid over the surface so fast, Karr couldn't tell exactly how she was pulling up the intel. He didn't know how these young recruits were so intuitively good with the touch screens.

A headshot of CH012SYTH-L came up. She had chin-length, dark-red hair and golden eyes in a thin face—a list of stats displayed on the right.

"Have you worked with her before?" He stood behind her, looking over her shoulder.

"No, I have not. Let's see. C.H.0.1.2. Codename, Ghost. Assembled out of the old Citizen Hill facility. She has been active for four years and two months. Her human age is nineteen years. She comprises of fifty-two percent human organs, making her ideal for infiltration. She has a processing speed of 4096 G. Her combat programs scored well above the hundredth percent, and she has completed all Tier-One Training."

"When did she complete ASP?" Karr leaned in, studying the screen.

"She completed the Assessment and Selection Program last December. Her most recent upgrade was in May, so she's operating on the 5.2.6 version, so that's good."

"Mission metrics?"

"She has a hundred-and-thirty-nine successful missions, zero protocol breeches, and two minor disciplinary actions, and it looks like . . ." Handler Meechum squinted at the screen, "they were both administrative in nature."

Commander Karr shook his head. "And where is she now?"

Handler Meecham's fingers flew over the screen again. "She first reported in thirteen minutes ago in sector 71. Her current position is right, uhm . . . here."

She tapped the screen a final time, and the satellite view zoomed in to show an overhead view of a run-down city street. It wasn't a real-time image, though.

"The operative has already infiltrated. We secured a sixty-eight percent facial recognition match for the target, but we lost contact before we could lock in the intel drop."

"So, she completed milestone one already," said Karr. "She works fast."

"I am due to call her if she doesn't report in the next fifty-six minutes."

"Splendid." Karr paused a moment. "Call me immediately when she checks in." He turned, then walked away.

"Yes, Sir."

3

CITIZEN HILL

"Brother Bless." Master Dunlam's shoulders relaxed. Head raised, he locked eyes with her target. "This is Citizen, the one whom we spoke about." The priest extended an arm toward her.

Julian Bless, or Snowball in her view, hung his crimson-colored robe on a hook. Under the thick garment, he had concealed a black, Kevlar-threaded sleeveless shirt that clung to his chest and showed slender but toned arms. He ran his hands over his thick black hair. The hood left it sticking out in all directions like a lion's mane.

Perhaps, his self-grooming habits make it worse, she

thought to herself, then noticed the soft shade of green encompassing his irises.

He stared at her. His shoulders squared. The visual outline of his face lit up in a red line in her Graphic User Interface vision. His file photo came up on the right side.

Hundred percent match. Julian Bless, it read below.

"Sister Citizen." His voice was low and gentle. "Welcome. Please, have a seat." He moved over to a desk.

She gathered the torn poncho in front of her and took the nearest chair. It looked the strongest of the three options, but that wasn't saying much. She hoped her weight didn't collapse the piece of furniture. Her reinforced cybernetic body made her several dozen kilos heavier than her skinny frame looked.

A 1580 Canine-Bot sat motionless next to the desk. It had the blue and white markings of the Federation Patrol and a stenciled number fifteen in blue on its shoulder.

It must've been from the 3rd Battalion, she mused over the information. *I haven't seen this model for a while.*

The dog replica robot stared straight at Citizen as if looking through her. It was the size of a typical

German Shepherd, only twice as mean and twenty times lethal.

"Don't worry." Bless stood in the open, crumbling doorway. "I broke the code on this one. He's on our side."

"Well, I don't trust the Federation Patrol." Citizen pulled the poncho around her upper body. "Or any of their bots."

"You shouldn't." Bless toyed with something in his left front pocket. "But this is no ordinary patrol Canine-Bot."

From the looks of it, the sleek object was a control device or possibly, a memory stick—she wasn't sure which, and her ocular implant couldn't scan through the Kavaler threads of his overlapping shirt.

"If you say so." She took a sample of his voice to start a base reading.

The target walked over and set his hand on the bot's head. "This is Sid." The robotic dog's head turned to look at its owner, the sound of gears buzzed in its neck.

Citizen's proximity scanner was reading for any Federation codes emitted from the bot.

No traces. This knowledge intrigued her. *Maybe this Bless guy really broke its code.*

"How does one break a Federation code?" Citizen

scanned the room, recording the scene for evaluation playback during the mission debriefing once the job was done.

Julian Bless smiled. "Well, we were all given different talents, that's for sure. And mine is hacking. It took me three tries. The first two bots we captured didn't work out too well."

"What if *this one* doesn't do too well?" She took in the Snowball's pale completion. Then her eyes zeroed in on his hair, which offered a sharp contrast to his skin.

"It's not an issue. Sid here has a completely new CPU and no Federation chips of any kind." He held her gaze, and it was as if his green eyes could see through the ocular implants into the circuits that made up her soul. Well, that was, if she had one. "Master Dunlam tells me you are new to our tribe."

"Yes, I've been in search of refuge for a long time." She wondered why his skin stayed so fair in the sun—why he didn't tan.

His smile stretched from ear to ear. "I'm sorry for your struggles out there. We're glad to have you among us." He looked just like his image, and his voice sounded like she had predicted from knowing the rest of his physiology. His eyes were different, though. They were softer than she had imagined.

He unbuckled the sword belt around his waist

without looking and laid it on the desk next to his datapad. "I assume Master Dunlam has shown you the barracks and the commissary?"

"Yes, he has been rather helpful." She gave a curt nod.

"And how long have you been out in the Autonomous Zone?" Bless sat on a chair.

"About two weeks, I think." Citizen chewed on the inside of her lip, simulating a touch of nervousness. "The Federation was going to arrest me."

"For what?"

"S-stealing." She bowed her head, breaking eye contact to simulate a hit of nerves.

"For who? Yourself?"

She shot a glance his way but remained silent.

Bless nodded his head. He had not taken his eyes off her. "It is tragic, yet heroic, what we will do to help others."

Citizen tilted her head. "How do you know I was stealing for others? I could've been doing it for myself."

"Maybe." Bless grinned. "But we Elysium naturally have empathy for each other. It's a human survival instinct. I believe you're a person who would risk life and limb to help others because you're a kind and compassionate person. And I *believe* you coming into our fold isn't mere chance.

No. I'm sure you're one of us." Bless leaned forward and stared. "I can see it in your eyes. You are human."

If only he knew how ironic that statement truly came across. She resisted the urge to smirk, then reprocessed the last couple of sentences he spoke.

What did the Snowball see?

"What do you mean . . . human? Of course, I'm human." An alert warning went off in her head. "I'm as human as you."

"Exactly. You're alive, like us. You're not an empty shell or a blind Federation follower."

A notification appeared in her GUI vision. She opened it.

The current conversation prompted a human philosophical phrase to pop up.

The text *'I think. Therefore, I am,'* displayed across the bottom.

She had programmed relevant historical and philosophical phrases to alert her if she fell into any complex human content that her CPU would have trouble explaining.

"I think. Therefore, I am." She held the Snowball's green, inquisitive eyes.

Bless nodded. "Exactly."

He's so inviting. Why am I drawn to this man?

"May I ask"—Citizen scooted forward in her

chair—"What is the meaning behind the ritual of each person touching the red stone?"

"Ah, yes." A small chuckle passed his lips. "The ceremony can often confuse new members. It is our Earth Dedication."

"Earth Dedication?"

"Yes." Bless paused, perhaps for effect. "The Life Stone is rare. It comes from a specific type of rock formed underneath the earth's crust. It was taken from the location Elysium was born."

"Born?" Citizen probed her memory archives.

"Yes. The ideology of Elysium started with only two people—me and Master Clark, our eldest member, whom you have not met yet. He's one of the seniors. As Elysium grows, so too does our territory. Each time we establish a new permanent settlement, we place the Life Stone on the altar, and each member, or part of Elysium, touches the stone and dedicates his or her life to defending and growing the new territory."

"I see." Citizen documented the information, dated it, and then filed it away.

"The stone is made from the earth." Bless motioned with both arms as if talking to a large crowd. "Like us." He tapped his chest and continued talking with his hands. "We are human. We are natural. We're not made of metal or plastic, or dura-glass. We're not formed from the institutions of the Federation like some datapad put together in a factory. We are alive." He clenched his fists and raised them above his head to emphasize the last word, 'alive.'

Citizen didn't understand completely. She knew humans over time favored rituals that included specific motor skills and sacred objects. She would have to learn more to understand fully, but she had to make Bless believe she was following him.

She nodded slowly and stared into his green eyes. "Yes, I see."

"Touching the Life Stone helps remind us of this," said Bless. "No matter what happens in the waste-land"—he pointed out the window—"We mustn't lose touch of our humanity. You are welcome to touch the stone anytime, even if it's before the next ceremony. It's packed away with the altar, but we can unpack it at any time."

"I will consider it," replied Citizen.

Bless' eyes narrowed. "I believe you've seen the light. I don't believe you came to us by mere chance. I believe you're here for a reason."

"And why do *you* believe so much about me?" Citizen scanned his frame but was unable to obtain a complete reading of his vitals.

"It is what I do." Bless sat back. "In Elysium, we

not only care for one another, we know one another. You don't become one with a group by being an individual."

There was something about his tone that mesmerized her. She could see how normal humans would blindly follow him. "Master Dunlam gave me the impression each person is free in Elysium."

The smile returned to his lips. "Of course, we are free. But no one is *in* Elysium," he said, drawing out the words. "Everyone . . . is . . . Elysium."

Another philosophical phrase popped up: *man is born free but is imprisoned forever.*

Not sure what that one meant—the words left her needing input. She would have to ask about that when the time was right.

Citizen nodded. There was something mysterious in his voice. She was intrigued. This terminology matched what the records had said. However, there was still something in his tone that didn't register. She knew this had to be something related to the human emotions.

Her internal RAM scanned through thousands of lines of code, trying to locate an intel match of his vocal inflection.

Why did he say I was human? It was the first time a human had told her that.

"I'm sorry, but I don't fully understand if you could explain—"

"Julian," a voice shouted from behind her.

Bless looked over her shoulder, and she turned.

"Gollum attack, sector four, it's bad!" The man's face was red, sweating, and showed clear signs of distress.

"How many?" Bless stood and reached for his belt.

"We don't know," the man said. "but it's a lot."

Sid's robotic eyes glowed as ruddy-red as the end of a blowtorch. The bot rose, then sprinted out the door.

Bless, Master Dunlam, and the messenger hurried out of the room.

They must have forgotten about Citizen, which was fine with her. In an instant, she was up, activating her proximity scan. The scan was already linking to the datapad on his desk. Just a few more seconds to establish a link, then she could begin hacking.

"Sister Citizen." Master Dunlam's voice startled her.

"Yes?" She turned to see he had come back.

"It's not safe here. Come with us."

"Sure." Falling in stride, she ran behind Bless.

The human was fast on his feet, and he had

already drawn his katana. Not knowing where they were going and not knowing where sector four was, she stayed behind them. Although Bless was fast for a human, she could easily outrun him with her carbon-fiber muscles. She intentionally kept her pace slow enough to look human.

Once down the stairs, Bless joined three others who were also running through the rubble-filled streets. One had a sword, and the other two had long staffs. They already left Master Dunlam.

She wasn't surprised. He wasn't the fighting type.

Citizen didn't want to reveal her two multi-bladed trench daggers concealed on her back in their custom upside-down sheaths.

Others joined them, weapons in hand.

She was impressed to see how quickly Elysium turned from silent monks into warriors.

"Breach on the north wall," someone shouted ahead of them.

"How many?" Bless yelled.

"More than ten," the same voice called back.

Citizen stopped mid-stride, stooped, then picked up a small piece of metal. It must have been part of a sign or something. Its jagged edge would work, but it wasn't long enough. But it would have to do for now. Not that she would need a whole lot more against Gollums.

Were there scabbies too?

Cries of humans and roars of Gollums could be heard. They were getting close.

She rounded a corner. There, in between the crumbling structures of an old city street, Citizen paused.

Her optic blinked on the figures.

She was expecting Gollums. But these weren't Gollums.

These were huge, hulking figures.

'Hostiles of unknown origins' blinked in her vision. She began calculating the speed of these things by their steps.

Extreme Mass. Intelligence level unknown. Engage at a distance: the message read.

Whatever they were, they were unknown. They had the same skin color as Gollums, but they were larger than any Gollum she had ever seen. These creatures were twice the size of a human.

She watched as one monster picked one of the Elysium guards off his feet by the neck.

The monster roared and punched the man in the face. His limbs went still. The beast then threw the limp body onto the asphalt.

Citizen wondered if the pause experienced in her read-out was similar to the shock or fear that humans experienced? She threw off her poncho.

"Gollum herd over here." It was Bless' voice, but he was lost in a sea of bodies.

She zeroed in on his location and ran to him. At first, she was going to protect him. But now, it looked like she was going to have to join in the fighting.

Sid jumped and latched onto a Gollum's arm with his metal jaws. The canine bot shook its head so violently, the giant Gollum stumbled, then stepped off balance. That same move would have taken a regular man clean to the ground.

A Gollum roared from around a corner and went towards Bless. The beast's massive arms reached up before swinging down.

Bless slid down to his knees and used his katana to slice the monster's leg as he slid by.

The monster's cry went from an angry attack to a roar of agonizing pain. It spun around to grab Bless, but he was already on his feet swinging in anticipation of the monster's arms.

The blade cut into the monster's hands, and it jerked back.

Bless was already running. A second man cut the creature in the back, and it roared in pain again. They must be used to fighting these beasts already. These people were quick and worked together.

It's impressive for a bunch of snowballs without a

chance in hell of getting their way, or so the Federation has stated on numerous occasions.

Citizen leaped onto a pile of rubble and launched herself off of one foot at the Gollum. She stuck her makeshift weapon into the base of the creature's skull with a crunch of bone and a slurp of flesh. The beast crumpled underneath her.

Bless, and another were already engaged with a second beast. These things were everywhere.

Katana in hand, Bless had already made one good slash to the Gollum's arm, but the beast disregarded it. Bless crouched and slowly side-stepped, holding his sword with both hands.

His partner swung a long piece of chain over his head, keeping the monster at bay.

Citizen calculated the time it would take for the next closest Gollums to reach them—thirty-one seconds max. Two attacking them at once would be too much. The man with the chain whipped his weapon at the creature's head.

The Gollum caught it with his good hand and pulled the chain. The man on the other end flew toward him. And the beast grabbed the human by the arms, opened his mouth wide, and bit into the man's neck.

The man screamed in pain, but there was no saving him. Bright red blood spurted into the air.

Bless was moving in. As the creature went in for another bite, Bless ducked and sliced his katana up and into the monster's armpit, releasing a stream of the monster's green blood.

The Gollum backhanded a fist at Bless, but he was already out of the way.

Citizen adjusted her gait. She would have to engage her flexor cables to reach her target quickly enough. Bless would see the non-human jump, but she had no choice.

Her flexor cables, which replaced her normal human hamstrings, engaged, and she shot into the air. Her weapon landed home just as the monster turned its head, leaving the piece of metal stuck in its eye.

She landed in a crouch. He was still alive, but not for long.

The Gollum desperately tried to pull the metal out.

Citizen grabbed the chain. And as she pulled it free, she saw it was modified with a sharpened piece of rebar on the end.

A very effective weapon. Elysium kept impressing her. *They are fighters.*

Bless made a jumping slash. His blade cut the monster's hand off at the wrist. The beast's other fist connected and knocked Bless to the ground.

Citizen swung the chain over her head and stepped back to the perfect distance. She let the end go, and the sharp point cut into his other eye.

The beast roared and tripped backward. That would have to do for now. Bless was still getting to his feet when the second Gollum closed in on him.

Citizen sprung off both feet, flew in the air over Bless, and then landed with a run—the chain weapon still swinging.

The Gollum hesitated.

Running, Citizen let loose the chain at the monster's face.

He reached up and blocked it with a hand. The end of the chain wrapped around his wrist, and he clutched it, staring at what he caught.

Citizen kept running full speed and slid feet first between the Gollum's legs. As she passed underneath its crotch, she dug her heels in and stood up, giving the chain a strong pull.

That tugged the monster's hand down in between its legs, almost tripping the beast.

She ran to the side and wrapped the chain against its leg. Two of the monster's limbs were now tied, and it was too confused to do anything.

She examined the creature's movements.

They're smart. But they aren't strategists.

Citizen jumped side-ways with all her weight.

The chain pulled its leg out from under it, and the beast went down with a crash.

A third Gollum was going to be in range in seconds.

She dropped the tangled chain, jumped, and unsheathed her double blades from their holsters in the air. She landed, straddling the Gollum. She had a foot on each side and a dagger buried into each side of the skull.

The beast jerked and went silent.

Bless, nearby, was on his feet, finishing off another creature.

Two more beasts ran at her. They were too close, and they moved faster than she had expected.

She sliced with her dagger. And the blade caught one of the creature's arms. She ducked and rolled, then she came up ready to swing. But the other monster was already behind her and grabbed her wrist.

He pulled her off her feet and bit into her arm.

His mouth was so large. It engulfed her forearm.

She felt her organic skin break, but her reinforced bone casing held. With quick precision, she stabbed her other dagger at the beast's neck, but it immediately let go, and her blade touched nothing but air.

She landed in a two-footed squat.

The beast jumped back with his hands on his mouth. A grotesque expression of confusion emerged on his face. It opened its jaw, then looked at her arm.

Citizen stood there, taking in the scene. *What's going on here?*

The monster backed away. It roared and held out its hand, palm up in a stopping gesture to the other beast that had started closing in.

The beast's posture slacked, and its shoulders dropped. They exchanged a few growls.

Wait. They are communicating with each other.

The one who had tried to bite her pointed to his mouth, then to Citizen's arm. Simultaneously, they dropped to their knees and raised their palms to her. They both let out a light growl and closed their eyes.

"Watch out," shouted Bless. "Behind you."

Turning around, she saw a third one ready to confront her. She bent her knees in attack position.

Then one of the crouching brutes roared, and the newest beast stopped. The newcomer's eyes shifted back and forth between his companions and Citizen.

Her non-verbal behavioral software reported they were scared of her but expressed joy at the same time. For a creature to exhibit these two emotions at the same time was unique. They were clearly communicating to each other she was not to be harmed, but why?

"What are they doing?" Bless asked.

"I don't know." They were obviously not going to kill her.

Citizen took their lapse in tactics and used it against them just as she was programmed. She ran up to the first two and sliced their throats with ease. She turned to do the same to the third one, but it was already running away with a screaming roar.

Another one attacked her from the left. She ducked its punch, spun backward, then swung her daggers in her hands into a reverse grip. She sunk both blades into the back of the creature's knees.

Planting her feet, she engaged her flexor cables, then used all her strength to yank the monster's leg out from under him. The beast landed with a thud.

Citizen had the daggers out and jumped into another somersault, landing next to its head, and then sunk one dagger into its neck.

She looked up. Bless stood there, motionless, jaws open. He was amazed at what he had just witnessed. But his human amazement was going to get him killed. Another Gollum was approaching from behind him.

"Get down." She swung the other dagger back

behind her head for a throw. "Get out of the way," she shouted, then threw the weapon.

Bless saw what she was doing and ducked. The dagger landed in the Gollum's neck, stopping the monster in his tracks. Its beefy arms clutched his throat. Blood gurgled out his mouth, and seconds later, he stumbled forward. With his last step and one final cry, its body slumped and fell back.

Bless stared at the beast that almost killed him.

"Stop gawking." Citizen pulled her first dagger free and walked over to the other creature. "And help me make sure they're dead."

She reached down, pulled her second dagger out of the creature's throat, then wiped the blood off on the sides of the dead Gollum's arm.

On edge, she scanned the area.

Two Gollums squirmed on the ground but were being finished off by the rest of Elysium.

Threats extinguished: her display read.

Looking up, she saw Bless staring at her. She flicked hair out of her eyes with a jerk of her head, then used the tail of her shirt to clean the blood out of the skull-shaped design of the dagger's hilt. With casual ease, she re-holstered the blades into her back sheath.

"Why did those three stop attacking you?" Bless approached.

"I don't know," said Citizen, with a layer of honesty. "The one bit my arm, then stopped."

Sid's gears buzzed and whirled in her ears. Without turning around, she knew the bot was trotting over to their position. The mechanical canine rubbed against Bless' leg, as if affectionately, which confused Citizen.

Bots don't show emotions, at least any that I've seen.

"That's gross," said Bless.

The bot's head was covered in green Gollum blood, and now, so was Bless' pant leg.

If the bot could smile, it would—she was sure of it.

The canine unit looked at Bless, awaiting his command.

As she moved, she knew Bless watched her, studied her. By this time, he would notice she wasn't sweating or breathing hard.

"I could have handled them myself." Bless' keen eyes continued to rake over her frame.

"Yeah, sure, maybe one, but you had a snowball chance in hell of taking them both down."

"So you say." He continued to study her. "Either way, thanks for saving me."

"You're welcome," said Citizen.

"You're quite the fighter." Bless wiped the blood off of his katana. "You're so good. You're almost supernatural."

She looked at him, and they locked eyes.

Yep. It's official, she thought. *He knows something but isn't going to say anything.* She didn't understand why yet. *Maybe he's being deceitful.* At this point, she didn't know if she could trust him yet.

"Are you guys all right?" One of the members ran up.

"Yes, we're fine," said Bless.

"What were these things?" Citizen knelt next to her last kill.

Bless kicked the leg of the closest one. "We call them Trolls. They're mutated Gollums. We started seeing them about a year ago. But lately, we've seen them in larger numbers. Their herds are growing." He used the tip of his sword to move one of the dead arms.

Citizen knelt next to the mass of crumpled, gray-ish-green muscle. She picked at one of the open cuts, examining the green blood on the tip of her finger. To the humans, it appeared she was looking at it. But internally, she was letting the blood secrete over the nano-receptors on the tip of her finger. Her CPU would analyze the cellular structure and bio-info. It would take several minutes.

"They strike strategically." Citizen rose, but she continued to survey the area. "They hit from different angles, then wait to attack when your back is turned."

"They're smarter, more strategic than we have ever seen a Gollum. And they are bigger, stronger, faster, and more aggressive," confirmed Bless.

"They don't appear to be mindless hordes." Citizen dropped her hand to make them think she was done with the blood. But she didn't wipe it off. She just let her nan-receptors process the material. She moved over to the creature's head to study its face. In a crouched position, she pulled up a dead eyelid and examined its eyeball.

Her T-581 ocular implant recorded the blood-shot iris and the shape of the eye. It recorded thermal imaging and infrared, as well as mapping the vein structure and nerve endings. She then moved down the arm and held its hand. It was heavy and twice the mass of hers. She flattened the over-sized digits with both of her hands and scanned the bone structure of the fingers.

"Is there more you can tell me about them?" She shot a glance his way.

Bless nodded and knelt to her level. "They seem to have a heightened olfactory system. They smell human flesh and devour it when they find it. We believe they have more advanced intelligence."

"How intelligent?" She examined the ear structure.

"They're smart enough to work together," said Bless, "smart enough to create diversions on our perimeters." He studied her face. "You don't show much emotion, do you?"

"And hearing?" There was a good chance he knew for sure.

"Yeah, that's enhanced, as well."

Citizen looked back at him just as the initial results from the blood scan popped up.

Trace amounts of Gollum DNA. Normal Human Levels. No match in the existing database. Further testing recommended: the report replayed twice.

"I bet they are the product of Gollum inbreeding."

Bless nodded. "I've been thinking that too. But we just need to get some blood samples to a lab. A real lab, that is, to confirm." He said it in a way that made Citizen suspect he knew what she did. "Although, if that's true, they're reproducing at an alarming rate."

"Do you have samples? Or do we need to collect some now?" Citizen called his bluff.

"We already have samples." Bless rose. "But the only facility that has tech like that is in New Therian."

"What were they doing when they stopped attacking me and fell to their knees?" She replayed the moment in her thoughts.

"I don't know," said Bless. "We've—I've never seen that before."

"Sir," the other man said, "we need to go."

"Collect all the weapons you can," Bless called out to the others who were already moving. "How many did we lose?"

"Eight dead, two wounded," the other man cast his gaze at the ground.

"Damn it." Bless let out a heavy sign. "Take their gear. We won't have time for a burning. We move out in three minutes." He sheathed his sword and walked away.

He's more like a military commander than a cult leader. And he's an impeccable swordsman.

Citizen kept her eyes on him and followed his every move.

4

JULIAN BLESS

"You okay?" Julian Bless studied Citizen.

She's different, changed, perhaps, or evolving.

Brown, knee-high boots covered her feet and shins. And she wore a gray top with ribbon-tied sleeves. Leather ran through the eyelets. Less than twenty-four hours ago, he thought this girl was just another refugee from the wasteland.

He was suspicious of her, just like any other new member. Then once they began fighting the horde of Trolls, he thought she was an incredibly gifted fighter. But now, he was almost positive she was a Sythy.

This was the third time he had formed an

opinion of her today.

No one can jump and move like that. At least, not the way she did without genetic enhancers and flexor cables. *Was she a Sythy?* Almost certain. *Could he trust her?* That was still to be determined.

"There they are." Bless settled down on the rock beside Citizen.

They had a good view overlooking the burning buildings and what remained of the village. Citizen had probably been studying them with her IR or night vision already. If she was a Sythy, she was doing a damn good job of blending in.

Sid trotted up and laid next to him.

"Yeah, I see them." Citizen laid belly down on top of the rocky slab.

Inches from her, he studied her up close. Her ribs and upper body moved with each steady inhalation. If simulated, she did a damn good job of mimicking breathing.

Bless peered through his night-vision goggles. There was a whole herd, all right. He performed an initial count of the Trolls. "There's at least forty of them."

Countless dead bodies were scattered around the walking horde. Some of the Trolls sat on their haunches eating human remains.

"And there'll be more by nightfall." Bless sighed.

He and his men had responded too late, and a reactive stance did nothing to protect this village. His heart ached. He wanted to save everyone. Bless, and his followers could only do so much. But this was unacceptable.

"What now?" Citizen rolled onto her side.

"We gotta move out."

She only nodded in response.

The Trolls were using the infected humans to collect the dead bodies.

"Looks like they're using scabbies as slave labor." It would be dark soon. They didn't have much time, and they definitely didn't have the manpower to launch an assault as he had initially planned.

"How many do you think are really down there?" Citizen turned her gaze to the horde once more.

Julian squinted into his binos. "There are usually about double the number below ground. Team Two said they got a good fifty or sixty on the other side of the village. So, we're looking at around two hundred, more or less."

"Two hundred of those things would tear through New Therian." Citizen stared into the distance as if she could see.

"Why'd you go with the skulls?" Bless' arm brushed hers.

"What?"

"The skull designs on those daggers of yours?"

"I found them," she said. "I like the skulls. They remind me of death. That we can die at any time." She paused a moment. "Why the katana?"

Bless shrugged. He didn't want to tell that story. "Practicality. It's the most effective."

Interesting. He took a deep breath of the early evening air. *She's trying way too hard to be human. And she's trying to change the subject.*

Julian knew what he had to ask and now was as good of a time as any. "Are you a Ronin, or did the Federation send you?"

Her head whipped towards him. "What?"

He stared into his binos like the question was completely normal, then turned to her.

"You're obviously a Syth-L." Julian lowered the binos. "But I think you're a Ronin." He pauses a moment, formulating his next words. "If the Federation sent you, you'd have killed me already."

Her red hair perfectly framed her face. Her golden-yellow eyes focused on him.

The sensitive lenses were probably recording every micro-expression and every slight change in the color of his skin for clues to help identify his emotions. Her eyes narrowed, but she remained silent.

She's a most curious distraction, he mused. *These new model Syth-Ls looked more lifelike than before.*

He knew Sythys had human organs, but he couldn't tell if her eyes were natural or not. It was as if she was hungry. He saw the same look on the people's faces who followed him.

They came to him for answers. They came hungry. And he provided sustenance.

But how could this Syth-L crave the same kinds of answers? There was something special about her.

"I had my suspicions," said Bless, "but when that Troll didn't bite through your arm, I knew. I've seen them bite off too many limbs of my people."

"So, you've seen them before, many times?" She avoided answering his question.

"Yes, and I don't think they have come across a Syth-L before."

"Why do you say that?"

"When that one bit you and stopped attacking, it was talking to the others. We have no way of understanding their speech. But it looked like they were in awe of you. Almost as if they were, well, worshipping you."

"That would make sense." She gazed out into the early evening twilight. "A primitive life form coming in contact with something exponentially advanced would be difficult to understand. Life forms often attribute spiritual qualities to things they don't understand."

Bless nodded. "They crave human flesh. And to come across something that looks human but clearly is superior like you would certainly cause them not to want to harm you. They would want to keep you, worship you, maybe even study you."

"So, I would be like their god." A smile rolled across her lips.

"Yeah, but they don't treat things like normal humans. They'd likely tear you apart, piece by piece, and then hand the little bits from their poles."

"Maybe being their god isn't such a good idea after all."

"Nothing about them is good." Bless adjusted the sword on his belt.

"Why does the Federation want you dead or alive?" Her question hit him like a slap in the face. "I am aware of the threat your group poses to New Therian leadership, but the amount of resources they've put into finding you indicates you have a much higher value."

Bless ran a hand through his mess of thick hair. *Value? What an interesting way to look at it.*

"I was the youngest member of the Microbiology Task Force."

The Sythy cocked her head to the side.

"*The* Microbiology Task Force? As in, the Federation program that lost the virus?"

"Not only did we release the virus, but we also created it."

She leaned back and nodded, taking in those words. "I see."

"Once the virus results escaped, and they shut the program down, they wiped away all knowledge of the project. They kept us under watch; my whole family was under surveillance. And they monitored all our codes and programs. It was like being under a microscope." Bless recalled those awful, fear-filled days.

"How did you end up out here?" Again, she expressed a most unusual need to understand, along with an unwavering curiosity.

Bless took in a breath, then let it out with a hearty sigh. He didn't want to drudge up the old feelings again.

But this Sythy was responding to honesty. So, he had to keep going.

"I broke ranks. I was the whistleblower. We eventually made a plan to leave. It took a while, but I escaped. Thanks to all my credits and some friends I knew in the academy, I made it to the Autonomous Zone. I've been *persona non-grata* to the Federation ever since."

"They've been trying to kill you?" A flicker of emotion swirled in her eyes.

"Yes." Julian nodded. "The only way to survive was to get off the grid. It's my mission to inform the people, so everyone will know the truth of what happened."

"And what is that truth?"

"The Federation thinks they can control everything. Even life through genetic manipulation."

"And what they can't manipulate, they extinguish."

"Exactly, but I cannot infiltrate New Therian without numbers. Now, with Elysium, I have a chance. And you"—he faced her—"you're perfect for Elysium. You have the compassion to help others."

"No, I don't. Compassion is an emotion."

"Compassion may be an emotion, but it is also knowledge."

She paused for a long time after that one. "Who else?" Her eyes held a curious expression, demanding an answer.

"What?" Julian asked.

"You said, we," said Citizen. "They were tracking your family too. What happened to them?"

Julian's face burned. "Not that." He couldn't talk about that. "Not now." Avoiding the question, he gazed out into the darkness.

He pursed his lips together, trying to squeeze away the pain. He let out a slow breath of air.

Breathe, just breathe. Don't think about that day.

Julian focused on his breathing to stuff the pain and anger deeper into his chest. He reached down and took a drink from his hydro-pack.

Relax. Relax. Change the subject. "We have to tell the others about this herd." He got up.

"You are not answering the question."

The Sythy still had a lot to learn about emotion. It was apparent she didn't want to go there.

Bless gritted his teeth. His hands clenched, and he started to sweat.

Just breathe. One breath at a time. He would not talk about it. *She didn't need to know, just like everyone else.*

"Why do you think I left?" He ran his hands through his thick hair. "Don't ask me about my family again."

"I do not understand. Your heart rate has doubled," said Citizen. "My sensors indicate your expression of anger is hiding an emotion of fear. And there's a 73% chance you're feeling sorrow right now. But you do not show it."

"You are a Sythy, then?" Bless grinned.

She looked at him. "Yes."

Julian looked away. "Humans are complicated."

46

"I have the latest approved field version of micro-expression interpretation available, and I still do not see a preponderance of evidence that you're deceitful. But all other indicators reveal you have conflicted emotions."

"I believe the people should be told the truth."

"Are you telling me the truth?"

"All of your high-tech sensors and software can't tell you if I'm lying?"

"None of them read a hundred percent."

"Well, we humans rarely feel something that's a hundred percent, so you may be more human than you think."

Julian rubbed his weary eyes, then took in a deep breath.

His temples throbbed in pain. He was getting less and less sleep these past few days.

"I no longer believe man was supposed to be in charge of human evolution. It didn't work. It will never work. Life isn't an algebraic problem that is waiting to be solved. Some things are meant to be mysterious, and others, we were never meant to learn or understand."

"If I'm from the Federation, why not just have your men or your dog kill me?" Citizen pointed at the bot.

Sid's gears buzzed. He tilted his head, and one ear

lifted.

"Well, I have no reason to kill you yet. For whatever reason, you found us. And you are worth a hundred fighting men. And besides, if I told anyone else, even I wouldn't be able to stop them."

"Stop them from what?"

"Disassembling you," Julian whispered. "If Elysium knew you were a Sythy, they would turn on you. The level of tech you possess in your body would be enough to hack into the Federation system and infiltrate them from the inside. Your body alone contains ten times the data we've fought five years to discover. And your tech would give us a fighting chance to overthrow the Federation and win this war."

"So, the Trolls want to disassemble me, and now, your people also want to rip me apart?" She looked away. "I think your people would have a hard time containing me."

Julian nodded. "We would lose a few, that's for sure. But remember, we're not a group of individual people. We are Elysium. We work together. We fight together."

"And you would all die together, Snowball."

Bless laughed. "You said that wrong."

"What."

"Snowball." He chuckled again. "Correct use

would be, *'You have a snowball's chance in hell of succeeding.'*"

"Perhaps, but I prefer to call you a Snowball—an anomaly of sorts." She paused a moment. "And to your point, Julian Bless, you and your Elysium followers have a snowball's chance in hell of taking me down."

"You are strong, no doubt, but enough bodies can eventually overpower even the strongest carbon-fiber muscles."

"So, why don't you kill me now?"

Julian looked through his binos again, watching the Trolls chain up another infected human. "I believe you are here to help us."

"And what if you're mistaken?"

"I hope I'm not." Julian shrugged. "That's what faith is all about. Call it a gut instinct. Although, I doubt your programming has reference points for human concepts like faith, belief, and hope. Unless you have some super-advanced emotion chip that I'm not aware of."

"So faith is the same as hope?" Her tone changed.

He was right about her. She seemed curious about humanity.

"Kind of, but not really," said Julian. "Faith requires one to believe in that which an individual cannot see."

"How can hope be kind of like faith but not really?" Her brows furrowed in confusion.

"Now, that's funny." A chuckle passed his lips.

"I do not understand."

"Exactly." *But you want to*, he thought.

How could he get a computer to understand the complexities of the human condition that humans themselves struggled to grasp?

"They are similar, and their meanings do cross-over, but at the core of their guts, they're not the same. Think of a Venn diagram—where parts of two circles overlap, yet they remain independent circles."

"I understand the definitions," the Syth-L said. "But they are still separate. How do humans overlap, as you say—or define?"

Honesty is what made Elysium what it is—what it shall always be. So, how does he now explain this to a non-fleshy?

"Well, to be honest, we humans don't really understand it. We just know it. We feel it in here." He tapped his chest where his heart was.

She's probably struggling to differentiate between the concept of the heart as a soul and the physical muscle. The thought made him chuckle.

Citizen looked as if she was still processing the information.

"What else do you know about these Trolls?"

Citizen turned back to look toward their prey. Her computing brain went back to logic, solving the next highest priority problem. It was always tricky talking with a Sythy.

"We've had a theory that it was inbreeding. But I don't think it stops there." Julian cleared this throat, then took another sip of water.

"What do you mean?"

"We raided an outpost about six months ago. It was a safe-house for Federation Patrols. There was one unit that was still transmitting when we broke the door down. I hacked in and stopped the decontamination before they destroyed the entire datapad. We extracted a gold mine of info. It took us a while to sort it all out."

"And?"

"Some of it we can never use, but there was one beneficial file. It talked about Project Goldfish."

"Goldfish?" Her brows arched into bows over her almond-shaped eyes.

"The file was incomplete, of course. But it described a secret genetic testing lab. We still don't know the location of this facility, but what we do know, they were doing DNA enhancements of Gollums, specifically."

"Only Gollum DNA?"

"Yes. The report said the strands were more

stable than anticipated but that all test subjects failed."

"Failed to do what?"

"We don't know. That's still a mystery," replied Julian. "Our best guess, with putting all the pieces together, it was some kind of roadmap to reverse-engineer the Gollum DNA. But since the subjects failed, we believe this to mean they mutated."

"Mutated into the Trolls?"

"That's right." A yawn escaped his lips.

"Do you still have this data?" Citizen held his gaze. "Can I see it?"

"Why would you want to see it?"

Citizen stared off into the darkness again. "Perhaps I can fill in some of the missing pieces."

Julian stared at her. "I never met a Sythy that didn't go by her serial number."

She stood and dusted off her pants, then turned away.

Julian sprung to his feet. He grabbed her arm, spinning her to face him. "Why are you here?"

She hesitated. "My story is complicated."

"As is mine." Bless swung his arm in the direction of the rest of the party behind them. "So are all of ours."

"I cannot reveal why I am here. But I can say I am not here to hurt you."

"Then, if the Federation sent you, what keeps me from alerting everyone else?"

"I am here to help," she said.

He didn't completely believe her. But why would a Federation Sythy be here and yet, not kill him?

She stared back at him for a long time. "My name is Citizen Hill."

"Citizen Hill? Like the township?"

"That's where I was born," said Citizen. "You fleshys are named after your parents, correct? Well, my parents were from a secret facility. A lab in Citizen Hill." She walked off.

Bless walked back to the group. Sid remained by his side.

The bot's metal claws clicked on the rocks.

I don't recall any Sythys giving themselves a name before.

He set out to find the three seniors, Clark, Dunlam, and Dester, who made up the rest of the advance party.

Citizen Hill was away from the group but then walked towards them once their voices met her ear.

"There's more." Bless kept his eye on her general location. "There's many more. Team Two said they're attacking towns all over the outskirts. This large herd is headed straight toward New Therian, and they're destroying everything in their path. They could reach the city as early as two days."

"How big is the herd?" Citizen approached and took a seat on a burnt stump of a tree.

"Two hundred"—Bless turned his attention on her—"maybe more."

Dester walked up, holding a makeshift spear. "We shouldn't talk here." He motioned his chin toward Citizen.

"She's fine." Bless waved off Dester's words of caution. "We can trust her. She saved my life. And she's good in a fight."

Dester glared at Citizen. "She's an unknown in the equation."

She looked back at Bless. "What happens when that heard reaches New Therian?"

"Nothing good, I'm sure." Bless shook his head.

"We must warn them," said Citizen. "They'll be defenseless."

"No." Master Clark raised a hand, then said, "We don't have to do anything because they—"

"No. We do have to." The ghosts of Bless' past echoed through his mind. "The formidable obstacle they'd pose to the Federation Leadership isn't worth the many innocent who would die." He adjusted the katana hanging at his hip. "Let's clean up. We move out at first light."

5

CITIZEN HILL

That night, after most of the fleshys had fallen asleep, Citizen crept out of the Elysium camp. HQ needed to know the intel she held, and as fast as possible, so she trekked to the tallest mound of rocks and began to climb. Halfway up the rocky formation, she turned on her night vision.

Heat signature sensors picked up no life forms in a hundred-meter radius.

At the peak of her perch, the signal strength went to ninety-eight percent. She stopped, then tapped into her voice-activated commlink. "Ghost to base. Ghost to base?"

"Go for base," the handler squawked over the channel. "Where have you been?"

"Shut up and listen. I don't have much time," said Citizen. "Objective one complete, I am in the group."

"Do you have the package?" The handler asked.

"Not secured, no. But I am with Snowball now— the package. But I have an urgent message."

"Stay on the mission," the handler said.

"Listen to me," said Citizen. "There's a threat to New Therian. A large herd of Gollum moving from the west. They'll reach the outskirts of the city in forty-eight hours."

"That's not a problem."

"No, these Gollum are different. There's a new breed that's twice the size and strength. They're fast and incredibly strong. They hunt and eat human flesh. And they're intelligent. If this herd reaches the city, there'll be nothing to stop them."

"What are you talking about?" The handler's voice went off-script.

Citizen pulled up the recording. "Send File V 2-4." She watched it play in her mini screen.

"Dear God. Contact the boss right away. Tell Commander Kerr we're under red alert," the handler relayed to someone nearby. "Ghost, stand by. Will send further instruction at the regular time."

"What about the package?"

"Hold one moment. The commander is on the line."

Citizen's com went silent. *Great. That's really helpful.*

Sixty seconds ticked by, then static returned to the line.

"Continue to Milestone Two," the handler said. "Isolate the package. He is to be taken alive."

"Repeat that?"

"New instructions." A layer of tension oozed through the communication, then ended as quickly as it filtered over. "Under no circumstances can he be killed. You must protect him until you deliver him to us. Once you are secure, transmit your location, and I will send a transport drone."

"But what about these large Gollum?" Citizen asked. "They could kill many innocent lives if they reach New Therian."

"Don't worry about that," the handler said. "Focus on the mission." The commlink squelched dead.

At the end of the conversation, the handler's lack of empathy was the opposite of Bless' voice.

Why was Bless so different?

Both of these people were human. Unless, somehow, the Federation was now using Syth-L handlers.

But that would be a waste of credits. Okay, on to more important things.

Citizen walked back to the camp.

Such as how to get Bless away from the group.

She didn't know why, but the destruction and death these Trolls inflicted created large amounts of distress in Bless. Not only was his increased consternation repeatedly confirmed by his voice inflections, but his skin tone and micro-expressions matched as well.

Why is he so emotional about these Troll attacks? Especially when the handler isn't. It doesn't make sense.

Bless was a warrior. He was used to this, and he knew the precarious nature of human life. If his file was correct, which it would be since the Federation had nothing to gain by giving her false intel. Why was this particular threat creating so much anxiety in him and the other humans that followed him?

This human, Bless, is peculiar.

She had not seen other humans follow someone with so much passion before. Even Federation troops didn't follow Commander Karr or Dr. Drayson like these people followed the snowball, the target, Julian Bless.

There was something about Julian Bless that all the record-scanning and computer power of her CPU could not place. When he interacted with his followers, he exhibited human emotions that she had no record of. She had not experienced gaps in her processing like this before. Maybe an emotion chip would help her decipher this unfamiliar data. She would request one after this mission was over.

The mission? Yes.

Why was she spending so much time thinking about things outside of her mission objective? Concerns of loss of human life unrelated to her mission never made her question anything before?

A growing desire to follow Bless, and his cause infected her like a virus. She had received satisfaction from helping protect these innocent people.

Her mission told her to extract Bless. But she couldn't let those Gollum-trolls reach New Therian.

But why think this way?

Her repeated conversations with Bless about compassion had not been helpful. In truth, it only made things more confusing. Obtaining more data from the snowball would help.

Now, back at camp, she laid down and pretended to sleep like she had been doing before her excursion. It was yet another human behavior she had to pretend she possessed.

6

Octavian Karr

"What is it? What did she find?" Commander Karr approached Handler Meechum and stood behind her, hands clasped behind his back.

"Just got the file, Sir," said Handler Meechum.

Karr had Meechum moved to a private control room after the Syth-L's last transmission. The last thing he needed were tongues wagging about classified information.

At her terminal, the handler's hands flew across the touch screen, hitting multiple buttons. A viewing screen popped up. One swift touch and it started playing.

"This is what she sent about twenty minutes ago,

Sir. I don't know what these creatures are." She tapped the screen. "They're like Gollums, but they're huge. Her data indicates this herd will reach New Therian in less than forty-seven hours."

Commander Karr watched the video.

he Syth-L's ocular lens had obviously recorded the data. It showed a group of humans fighting with a small band of 2.0s.

"Stop," said Commander Karr. "Go back. Who is that?" The Commander pointed to a man swinging a sword in the foreground. The handler reversed the video. "Is that the package?"

"Yes, Sir," the handler said. "That's Julian Bless. Package contact confirmed."

Commander Karr stepped back. "So, she has found them—him."

"Yes, Sir. The file looks like she did a blood analysis of one of these creatures. She also sent multiple files of physiological data, bone measurements, all kinds of data."

"But she has not given an extraction time, has she?" Karr paced the floor in a three-foot radius.

"No," the handler said. "In fact, she has made repeated warnings about the humans that would die if this herd of large Gollums attacked New Therian."

"That's odd." He smoothed the neck of his collar.

"How can she bypass mission protocol by not requesting an extraction window?"

Handler Meechum touched the screen again, and her finger scrolled the display to read over lines in a manual. "The only way I know a Syth-L can override mission protocol is if the original protocol compromises the safety of a package. At that point, she has to shift."

"Explain yourself."

"Yes, Sir. She cannot allow an injury to occur to the package, even if that prolongs the mission. So technically, she's not bypassing protocol. She is finding a way to fulfill both the mission and protect the package. She's a clever one."

"Well, I'll be damned." Karr leaned back. "She's done it." He turned on his heel, then walked away.

Twelve minutes later, he headed toward Dr. Drayson's conference room.

Pausing outside the door, he straightened the buttons of his gray uniform, then took in a deep breath. He was tardy, but he needed the extra time to collect the data before he spoke. Heartbeat slow and under control, he strolled in with purpose.

Inside the bleak, gray room Representative Bachus sat next to Dr. Drayson, sucking up as always. The doctor sat at the head of the table, and four other Representatives were already seated.

"Commander Karr, thank you for joining us." Dr. Drayson pointed to the only empty chair in the room.

No one said a word until Karr sat down.

Dr. Drayson's white hair was slicked back like always. He peered down his long nose. His steely eyes and sunken cheeks gave him a sickly look that would have killed most men. "And what is your report of the operation?"

Commander Karr cleared his throat and sat up straight. "Approximately three weeks ago, a new faction moved in the Autonomous Zone. The group calls itself Elysium. They appear to be some kind of rebel cult. Their leader is Julian Bless."

"Bless? Our Julian Bless?" Representative Bachus, elbows on the table, leaned forward as if to soak up each word.

"Yes," confirmed Karr.

"We should have exterminated that whistle-blower when we had the chance." Representative Bachus let out a heavy sigh.

Karr continued, "This Elysium cult has declared ownership of sectors fifteen through twenty-nine and shows no sign of slowing."

"How many are in this group?" One of the other Representatives, a woman with similar hair, slicked back as Bachus', chimed in.

Karr recognized the woman but didn't know her name. "About a hundred-and-thirteen people. Last week, we assigned a Syth-L to infiltration. We had actionable intelligence that indicated one Julian Bless was operating inside sector nine. The Syth-L's mission was to locate Julian Bless, infiltrate his band of followers, arrest him and bring him in, dead or alive. As of today, she has successfully infiltrated his people and made contact with Bless himself."

"We should assassinate him immediately." Representative Bachus was a hawk in the most extreme ways. He glared at Karr with his deep-set eyes. There was nothing but disdain in his face.

Karr lifted a finger. "That was not the directive." He paused a moment, then continued, "And now, the order is to extract him alive at all cost."

"Why? Julian Bless is the one man that could expose the origins of the virus." Representative Bachus pointed his finger and jabbed it on the table. "If the people find out what he knows, there would be a large-scale revolt from numerous sectors. Not even our private troops could stop a full-force rebellion. Why take the chance? We should just kill him now and get it over with."

"Because it appears we've just learned some additional information," said Dr. Drayson, nodding to Karr.

"Yes, Sir," confirmed Commander Karr. "This morning, our Syth-L sent DNA evidence of the 2.0s along with this video." He motioned to the screen on the wall, and the same clip of Bless fighting the Gollums played with no sound.

"And how many 2.0s did they encounter?" Representative Bachus sat, wide-eyed, gaze glued to the screen.

"She said there was a small group of thirteen initially. That's what you see here. But she also sent a video of a herd numbering close to two hundred approaching New Therian from the western hills."

"Two hundred? That's impossible," said another Representative.

"She sent the thermal scan data as evidence, and satellite imagery confirms," said Karr.

"If this Syth-L has proof that the 2.0s exist, we have a major problem," Dr. Drayson's deep voice shuttered through the room. "If they leaked this to the public, Operation Goldfish, the existence of the 2.0s, along with the knowledge of what Bless already has about the Microbiology Task Force, this could be unrecoverable for the Federation." The doctor rested his chin on his hand.

"How did she find the 2.0s?" Representative Bachus' knee bounded under the table.

"This was most unexpected," said Karr. "We had

no idea any Gollum 2.0s were near those sectors. And to have such a large herd can only mean they're reproducing at alarming rates. Rates too great for our forces."

"Does anyone else in the city know about the 2.0s?" Representative Bachus shifted in his seat.

"No. Only the handler assigned to me," said Karr.

The men looked at each other out of the corner of their eyes. Then their gazes landed on Dr. Drayson. His stoic expression was the same as always. His face didn't move, but his beady little eyes were concentrating.

"Do we have any other assets inside Bless' group?" The Representative poured water out of a silver-lined crystal decanter into a frosted goblet.

"No." Karr shook his head.

"I'm afraid Option A is no longer our best course of action." Dr. Drayson rolled his chair closer to the table. He folded his hands in front of him on rested elbows. "With Commander Karr's new intelligence, I'm afraid we are going to have to eliminate Option A."

"And do what?" Representative Bachus smacked his hands against the table, creating a thunderous boom in the room.

"We will have to move forward with Order 505," said Dr. Drayson. "And Doomsday Protocol."

The room went silent. Everyone looked at each other. "That will cost the Federation plenty of credits," said Representative Bachus. "There is a significant, uhm, investment we have in our assets."

"I am aware of our investment," retorted Dr. Drayson. "But we have no choice. It must be done."

Commander Karr leaned forward. "Are you sure, Sir?"

Dr. Drayson nodded his head with the power of a commanding yell behind it. "Absolutely."

"Yes, Sir, understood." Commander Karr rose, then pushed in the chair. "I will tell the handler to expedite the mission."

With the nod of Dr. Drayson's head, the meeting was over.

Karr was thankful to get out of the room. Once he did, he made his way back to the handler's control room. He would release the drone when and as ordered.

7

CITIZEN HILL

Citizen Hill stood next to Bless. He had his katana drawn. Her weapons remained snug in their sheaths, resting on her back.

She and Bless were on the edge of a small group of Elysium fighters.

His skills and ability to work together with others continued to impress her. Joining forces, they were about to defend a small valley between the outskirts of town and a massive hill.

The Elysium tactics of choosing such a strategic spot forced the Trolls to bottle-neck themselves. The humans were killing them one by one. If she could just move them a little farther down the hill, she could isolate herself and Bless from the main group. But Bless' people were excellent fighters and used to fighting melee style.

Things had been going as planned until a handful of Trolls ran up behind them, disrupting the strategic battle plan in place. Somehow, the beasts had gotten around the hill.

Three Trolls ran at them, and Citizen grinned. This could be the break she needed to separate Snowball from his flock.

Bless drew his sword and engaged one. Sid jumped and clutched the throat of another. With her daggers out, Citizen ran to the third. Its eyes met hers.

The massive beast swung like it was hitting a regular fleshy. She dodged the blow under it. She was already swinging up under his arm as she slid behind him. The blade sliced through the thick muscle and arteries of his armpit.

Anticipating his turn around, she dropped to her knees just in time. She sprung up too quick for him, and her other dagger lodged under his jaw.

Two more within range, both attacking at the same speed, closing in on her from opposite directions.

"Well, now, aren't you boys strategic?" Instead of waiting to get smashed, Citizen ran at the one to her right. "Too bad you two charge like a hunting pack of wild animals."

With one step, she soared into the air, then spun sideways over his head. Double daggers came down in a reverse grip, both stabbing into his shoulders on either side of his head. She swung her body around and landed on his back. The two monsters were still running toward each other. The one she was riding on was so big. He couldn't stop his momentum even as he was dying.

Ripping the blades out, she severed both carotid arteries, then pushed herself off his back with her feet. She flew in the air again over the second one. The two Trolls collided behind her. The one that wasn't bleeding expressed confusion as to where his prey went. And he remained dazed from smashing into his companion. He looked over his shoulder and shook his head.

Bless ran in and took off its massive head with one perfect slice from his katana.

Citizen back-rolled off and landed. Flicking the daggers into the air to fling the blood off her blades, she scanned for the next target.

Sid had already ripped the throat out of his first kill and ran after a second. Green Troll blood covered the bot's white and blue metal.

Tension filled her like never before. She wanted

to stay and help, but she had to complete her mission.

"We can get around behind and flank them if we go over this hill," Citizen yelled to Bless, who was right behind her.

Now the main line of Trolls was between them and the rest of Elysium. Her plan had worked. This was it. She was almost at the top when she realized Sid was running after them.

Damn. I didn't expect the dog to be along for the ride.

It followed Bless everywhere. When they reached the top of the hill, they were in a perfect flanking position.

"There's too many," shouted Citizen. "We have to wait."

Sid took off after the closest Troll.

Good. The dog was out of play now.

Julian stopped. His chest heaved.

Well, now is as good a time as any.

She switched gears and surveyed the area, ensuring meddling eyes weren't in range.

"Why?" He asked. "What for? Let's go."

"Sorry about this, Snowball." Citizen stepped behind him and grabbed the wrist that held his sword.

Before he knew what was happening, her other arm found his neck. Wrenching the sword from his grasp, she let it fall to the ground, tightened her grip on his neck, then squeezed.

"What are you doing?" Bless struggled, but it only took seconds for him to pass out from the lack of blood flow. He went limp, and she laid him down gently.

She removed his belt, sheathed the sword, and put the weapon over her shoulder. Then, with ease, she picked him up and sprinted to the rendezvous point. Her carbon muscles pumped.

"Ghost to base," she said, sparking the commlink alive.

"Base here, go ahead," the handler's voice squelched.

"Snowball confirmed. I repeat, the package is in-hand and en route to the rendezvous point."

"Copy, Ghost. We have your position. Transport drone is three minutes out."

Citizen reached the destination point. Her sensors picked up the drone's signal. It was close.

She laid Bless carefully on the ground, and he began to wake from all the movement. There was no need for restraints. The nano-net would be here soon.

Bless' eyes opened, and he sat up, confused. "W-what? What happened?"

"I'm sorry, Snowball." Citizen glanced at him,

then peered into the distance in search of the transport.

"There it is again, Snowball? So, is that my assigned target name?"

She ignored his probing question.

He instinctively reached for his sword that was usually on his belt, but he grabbed nothing but air. His eyes soon followed, and he saw that he had no weapon.

"Why are you doing this?" He asked in a daze.

'Incoming drone in twenty seconds' displayed on her vision screen.

"I'm sorry, Snowball—Julian Bless," she said. "My mission wasn't to kill you. It was to arrest you."

Bless' eyes widened at the realization. First, he heard the drone, looked around for it, and then he saw it.

"Citizen, you can't do this."

As she suspected, he didn't run, perhaps, because he knew she would catch him in only a few steps.

"This is how it has to be," she said.

"No, you don't have to do this."

"It's my mission." She turned to face him.

"Humans don't have missions." He held her gaze.

This made her pause. She thought about the statement.

What did the snowball mean?

Then the incoming alarm went off.

Drone approaching: the text blinked in the bottom of her GUI vision.

There it is, a mid-sized transport drone.

Citizen sighed, but she wasn't sure why.

It was a box-shaped container about the size of a compact car. Four enormous helicopter rotors spun from its roof. The engines whined as it flew closer. Dust kicked up, and the vehicle hovered about ten meters away.

Bless shielded his eyes from the dust and blowing sand. His mess of hair blew in all directions. There was nowhere he could go. The drone lined up with them, and the bay doors slid open. The nano-net gun came to life and pointed outside at its target.

"Citizen, they'll kill me," he yelled over the sound of the engines. "You and I both know this to be true."

She just stared at him. The micro-expressions she captured were new. He continued to surprise her with emotions.

With a mechanical burst, the nano-net cable shot out and engulfed Bless. He threw his arms in front of his face on instinct. The nano-cable divided and separated itself into multiple strands, just as she had seen it do many times before. Then strands separated and melted together as needed to create a pliable netting around Bless' body.

As Bless struggled, the strands settled around his ankles first, then his wrists—pulling them and binding them behind his back. Now that he was immobile, the strands melted back into one cable that retracted Bless' body into the container.

He kicked his legs, but all it did was cut a deeper path in the rocky dirt.

"Don't let them take me," he yelled as the darkness of the interior of the container swallowed him.

Again, his vocal inflection contained more than fear. It was something else. Sadness, maybe. She would review the audio later. The doors would close, and the mission would soon be over.

She held up the sword that still hung around her shoulder.

I should make sure they get this too.

She didn't want to leave it in the container with the snowball, just in case.

The doors should close. The drone should lift off by now. She looked up.

The doors were still open. Bless lay bound inside.

Why isn't it leaving? Then she saw it. The nano-gun was pointed right at her.

Her reflexes were fast but not quicker than a nano-gun. The net knocked her over as the nano-tech strands pulled at her and bound her hands.

"No," She shouted. Why would they be capturing her too?

Something must be wrong.

She engaged her carbon flexors to break free from the nano-tech. But it was like trying to split water. The strands were already forming complex bonds around her ankles and wrists. And in a matter of seconds, it pulled her into the container.

"Ghost to base," she called over the commlink. Nothing but static. "Ghost to base. The drone has malfunctioned. It's trapped me inside with the prisoner. Base, do you read me? I'm inside the drone with the acquired target—Snowball." She saw the hundred percent icon in the corner that proved her transmission was getting through. But there was no answer—only silence.

The cable pulled her into the dark container alongside Bless, who was already bound and lying next to her. The doors slammed shut before she could wiggle up.

Darkness swallowed her. The cables continued to retract and re-form around her.

The Nanos detected the weapons on her body, her two daggers and Bless' sword. The strands pinned her arms to the sides of her body, just out of reach of all three weapons.

"Snowball." Bless' voice echoed in the square,

metal box. "Seriously, that's the codename the Federation gave me?"

"No." She felt the drone liftoff, and the sound of the engines went into high gear. "It's the name I gave you along with the other snowballs living clueless as to how society runs. They just went along with it."

They were flying back to New Therian and into the hands of the Federation Leadership, back to Commander Karr and Dr. Drayson himself. What would they do with her—to him?

"Fine, Snowball, it is." A chuckle slipped from between his lips. "Well, just so you know, I'm glad I'm not the only one mislead by today's surprise capture."

Citizen engaged her night vision and looked over.

His face had gone from fear to a smile. A glimmer of humor played in his eyes.

"There must be a bug in the system," said Citizen. "Or one of the new handlers programmed it wrong. Told it to catch two prisoners instead of just you."

She struggled against the strands that hardened into solid metal enclosures all around her hands.

Damn. I can't even move a finger.

"I doubt it," said Bless.

"What do you mean?"

"Your mission was to capture me, correct?"

"Yes, and I just completed it." She paused a second. "Are you not captured, Snowball?"

"Oh, most definitely thanks to you." He scooted to a sitting position, inches away from her. "If they wanted to capture me so badly, it must mean I have something they still want. And that thing, you must know as well."

"What?"

"Now you know about the Trolls. They can't let that information get out. Think about it. After extracting the information they want, they will kill me, then dismantle you."

"They don't kill their own Syth-Ls." Citizen took a reading of his vitals. "They paid too much money to have me made." But the readings confirmed he was truthful, at least from what she could ascertain.

"I'm sure they thought of that and weighed the consequences." Bless let out a heavy sigh. "But how much would it cost them if you were to release all the data and recordings you now have in your CPU to the public?"

Citizen now understood. She was a pawn in a chess game, an expendable piece on the board.

She saw Bless' mouth curl down and his eyebrows stretched together.

The confused and empty thoughts she had inside

her now must be what disappointment felt like to a fleshy.

This human had calculated all the possibilities and the strategic consequences of the damaging data she now held. The Snowball was right. She would have given the same order in their place.

Immediately, she killed the commlink, and her internal GPS and navigation program captured in the drone. She could at least kill her signal.

"They betrayed me." The thought confused her further.

"Yes, they did. Just as you betrayed me."

"That's different."

"How is it different?" Bless scoffed.

She did not have an answer or no time to waste. She had to break out of here before the transport reached the Federation HQ landing pad in New Therian. Which would be approximately seven minutes at the speed they were flying.

"Can't you use your Sythy strength and break us out of here?"

"No." She resisted the urge to roll her ocular implants the way she'd seen humans do in the past out of sarcasm. "The nano-tech cables are too strong. They design the density for this very reason."

She scanned the generator controls. Her hacking code was scanning all frequencies. Maybe she could shut down the engines or hack into the navigation computer. But they blocked everything from her. Nothing was getting through.

"Can't you use one of your internal scanner things and take over the drone?"

"Already tried that. They shield all frequencies. No encryption is possible with my capabilities. There's nothing I can do, Snowball."

He shot her a disapproving look at her name choice.

She was able to see that the drone's computer code did have the orders written in basic programming.

Objective: Capture and retrieve Julian Bless and CH012SYTH-L 1: it read.

It was true, and there was no mistake. They had betrayed her. So, not only did humans want to disassemble her for parts, the Trolls wanted to worship her, and now, the Federation wanted her dead.

"So, we have no other choice?"

"No other viable options. Believe me. I just ran through all of them." She listened to the hum of the drone's engines. "We'll have to wait until we land."

"What other sensitive information do you have?"

"Nothing directly connected to this mission." She butted the back of her head against the metal transport. "Those bastards."

"I can second that statement." He grinned with an understated laugh. "You aren't like any Sythy I've ever met."

"Well, Snowball"—she held his gaze—"You're not like any fleshy I've ever encountered."

Her only logical option to survive was to wait until they landed and were extracted, then either try to reason with her captors or fight her way out once the nano-cables released her. But that was only if they released the cables, which they surely would *not* do. They knew what she was capable of. After all, they had designed her.

"So, what are we going to do?"

"Nothing. There is nothing to do. Why do you ask?"

"There's always a way out," said Bless. "We can't give up hope yet. I'm sure something will come up."

There's that word again. Hope. She still didn't understand what Bless meant by it.

Sure, she knew the definition. But she couldn't connect how this feeling of hope tied to a person's emotions and brain.

"Humans are so complicated."

Bless opened his mouth to say something, but the drone crashed to a stop.

She slid forward, then her head crashed against the side of the container, followed by Bless tumbling into her. Then the nano-stands adjusted both of their positions.

"What's that noise?" Bless' voice rose above the sound of the engine.

The drone hung in the air, sped up again, then smashed into something solid. This time, it spun in the air several revolutions, then stopped to hover once more.

"What the hell is it doing?"

Citizen read all her instruments. "I do not know. It shows we're positioned on the western border of New Therian. We're in sector fifty-two." It felt like the drone repeatedly crashed into the side of a building.

"We've just crashed into something else," said Bless, next to her ear. "Could we have hit a mountain or a wall?"

"It would never hit a mountain," said Citizen. "And we're too high for buildings."

"We ran into another drone then. In mid-air?"

"Extremely improbable." Citizen tried to get a feel of the direction the transport was going.

It increased altitude for another minute. Then the drone stopped, spun three-hundred-and-sixty degrees, then began decreasing altitude to a landing speed.

"Are we landing?"

"I think so." Citizen listened to the whine of the engine changing gears.

What is going on? The momentum slowed again, and the transport landed with a jolt.

Citizen and Bless bounced. Bless winced in pain. And if Citizen was human, the impact would've engaged the pain receptors in her back and neck.

Dust settled. The engine died down, but it didn't power off.

She heard nothing outside. No landing party to meet them. No Federation Troops. This was strange indeed.

Then her scanners picked something up.

"Hold on." She listened to every sound ruminating around her.

"What is it?"

"The drone is scanning all possible frequencies." Confusion made her circuits whirl. "It's troubleshooting."

"Can you hack it now?"

"No, it's still shielded. But switching frequencies is a last resort method," said Citizen. "It's requesting location coordinates. It has repeated its request to HQ over a dozen times already. It's as if HQ went silent. It has to find its orders. If it has no orders or no way to solve its problem, protocol default is for the drone to land and wait."

"How long does it wait?"

"Why do you ask, Snowball?"

"Well, unlike a Syth-L like you, I'm human," said Bless. "I will die without water in three days."

Citizen thought about his words. It must be scary for a bound human, locked in a metal container in the middle of nowhere with no access to food and water. If scared, Bless didn't show it.

Something crashed into them again. This impact was smaller than the last one.

They were still on the ground, and something repeatedly clanged into the container. It sounded like someone was hitting a metal box with a sledge-hammer. The noise rang.

Bless winced in pain from his ears, and Citizen turned down her audio sensors.

A minor explosion made her ears ring, then seconds later, buzzing noise hummed at a steady cadence, then the container stopped moving. The rotors whined to a halt.

No sound. Her scanners saw all data from the drone cease.

Then the metal doors buzzed to life and slid open.

Sunlight blinded her.

The nano-strands around her hands and ankles dissipated. She was free.

Scrambling to her hands and knees, she crawled to the opening with Bless right behind her.

She rolled out and landed in a crouch, ready to face Federation soldiers.

"Heads up." She unsheathed Bless' sword and threw it to him.

He was ready and caught it. "Got it." Bless turned around to face any attackers from the rear.

Citizen pulled her daggers and stood in a fighting stance.

All she saw was a wasteland. No one was there. No soldiers. No other drones. She looked around. Some disheveled buildings lay nearby. They were undoubtedly at the outskirts, as her GPS indicated.

Bless laughed. His sword was down.

"Why are you laughing, Snowball?"

Has he gone mad, she wondered? But a quick scan showed he was in optimal health despite the crash.

He continued to laugh at something on the other side of the drone.

She stepped next to him to view what he saw.

Sid stood there with the central controls of the drone held in his mouth. He had attacked the drone and tore out its vital components. The canine bot dropped the parts, and its false tongue hung out of his metal mouth, mimicking the actions of a real dog. Its mechanical tail wagged back and forth, and its gears buzzed.

"Good boy, Sid." Bless set his sword down at his feet, then held his arms out.

The dog sprinted to him and put both front feet on his owner's chest. "Ha, I knew you'd come!"

Citizen replaced her daggers in her back holster.

Sid jumped down and walked to Citizen and tilted its head.

"Thank you, Sid." She simulated a smile, and Sid wagged his tail in excitement.

"Well, now we have to get out of here," said Bless.

He was correct. If they knew they lost their precious cargo, they would come.

We. He said 'we.' Bless was her enemy. But now, all logical strategies indicated she had to work with him.

One of the human philosophical quotes displayed on her vision, '*the enemy of my enemy is my friend.*'

She scanned the area, overlaying the terrain with the maps stored in her database.

"The Federation Leadership will send more drones." She calculated the best path down the mountain.

But she couldn't help wondering why the transport had stopped? What had they crashed into? She looked in the direction they were traveling, toward New Therian.

There it was, the answer. The earth broke open in front of both her and Bless.

A large iron base plate protruded out of the ground. And from within the iron base, a massive, thick piece of dura-glass shot straight up into the air like a glass wall. It must have been at least three meters wide.

The entire structure continued north and south until it disappeared into the horizon.

She looked up. The dura-glass stretched higher than she could see, creating an impenetrable wall around the city.

"What is this?" Bless looked around, then his gaze fixed on the wall.

"It's part of the Doomsday Protocol," said Citizen. "It's a last-ditch measure to save the city from infection. The Emergency Action Plan. A mandatory quarantine."

"I've heard of the Doomsday Protocol," said Bless. "So, it's true. They can seal off the city. The entire city."

"Correct," said Citizen. "Someone must have made a mistake and activated the Doomsday Protocol. They probably didn't know how long it would take. The walls must have reached height before the drone made it inside. Cut off from communication no doubt caused the confusion."

Citizen unbuckled Bless' sword belt and handed it back to him. "I guess you'll need this."

He sheathed the sword and then put on the belt.

Audio coming from the south made her ears perk. Human voices. Engines.

"What is it?"

"We have to get out of here," said Citizen. "They're coming for us, Federation troops, dogs, at least one drone."

Citizen Hill and Julian Bless took off running into the wasteland. Sid stayed right behind them.

8

JULIAN BLESS

Julian Bless kept running. Citizen was already far ahead of him, and Sid was behind, bringing up the tail. The thought of this unlikely trio he found himself in brought a smile to his lips. He was strong and had been fighting for his life for years, but there was still no way he could ever keep up with the Syth-L. Her cybernetic components made her almost unstoppable.

But he had to keep going. It wasn't safe to stop yet. Together, they had started out running away from the edge of New Therian, but they were leaving tracks in the sand.

Luckily, Citizen had led them to a rockier area,

so at least now, they weren't leaving tracks for those hunting to find them.

The Federation troops were on foot. But the drone was the biggest problem. Bless could hear the winds of its engines but couldn't see it.

And speaking of seeing, where the hell did she go? He ran, looking around for any trace of her.

Citizen stepped out from behind a large rock.

Bless, trying to stop, had two choices, ram her or the stone formation. So, he chose the lesser of the two and slammed into the rock.

He groaned, then fell to his knees. Rolling over, he sat and rested his hands on his lap. He was sweating, and his chest heaved up and down.

"The Drone is two minutes away," said Citizen. "We have to make a stand here."

"How?" Bless ran his fingers through his sweaty hair, then stood up, putting his hands on his hips. He was breathing so hard. He could barely get the words out. "What are we going to do against a drone?"

"I have my beacon off. The drone won't be able to lock onto my heat signature as long as I'm far enough away," said Citizen. "I'll attack it after it locks onto you, down there." She turned and pointed behind her back, revealing a deep ravine. "You have to get down there, give yourself up, and

I'll attack the drone from above. That's our only chance."

"What?" Bless couldn't believe it. "I just survived one drone, and now you expect me to get captured by another, intentionally?"

"We don't have any time to argue, Snowball," said Citizen.

"I think it's growing on me."

"What? Do you have a parasite?" She approached him.

"No." His lips spread into a wide grin. "Your pet name for me. Snowball."

Sid trotted up and cocked its head sideways, trying to figure out what was going on.

"Sid, you go with him. Go, now. One minute thirty-two seconds out and counting."

"Dammit." Bless edged closer to the ravine and looked down.

Snowball, he replayed the single word over and over again in his head. *Why that word out of so many others?* Once things calmed down, he needed to find out why she chose that word out of all others.

Was it her choice—her idea or someone else's? The thought intrigued him on many levels.

The cliff edge he was on fell off into a canyon with a dry riverbed at the bottom. The surface wasn't just rock. It was dirt and had a slight slope. It wasn't straight down, but there was no way to climb it either. "How am I supposed to get down there?"

"You'll have to slide. Now go." Citizen ran off toward one of the larger rocks.

Bless gulped and looked down again. The sloping wall had to be at least fifty yards.

"Well." He glanced at Sid. "I guess we don't have much choice, do we, buddy?"

Sid's gears whined. He peered back in the direction the Drone was coming from. It was much louder now. The canine bot's attention returned to Bless, and he walked to the edge, sniffing, using its nose sensor at the edge of the canyon.

Nimbly, it slid its forepaws over the edge, stuck its hindquarters up in the air, and slid down the steep slope.

Bless watched the mechanical dog slid a few feet. Sid started gliding faster, gaining momentum, then he must have hit a rock with his paw because he yelped, flipped up, and then over. He landed in a self-contained ball, rolling.

Sid's metal claws dug into the dirt for traction, but he was going too fast.

Bless lost sight of him in a cloud of dust. Glancing over his shoulder, he looked back and saw the silhouette of the drone on the skyline.

"Damn." He didn't know where Citizen was or if he could trust her plan or not.

After all, she had just choked him out and captured him a little while ago. But she was right. He had no choice. Sitting down, he slowly let himself slide over the edge. His body fell, and he slid on his bottom. When he tried to slow himself down, dirt and small rocks caked under his fingernails.

Dust flew in his face, and he slid faster and faster. A third of the way down, he sprawled out, feeling the burn of the ground on his back. His shirt bunched up over his neck. He drew his katana and turned his body just before he lost control. The blade stuck into the earth, and he held all of his weight on the handle.

The blade sank deeper with his mass, and he slowed.

Now facing the wall, he straightened out his legs, and he braced his feet by digging his heels into the wall.

He kept sliding, still way faster than he wanted, but at least he wasn't falling as the incline turned away to a straighter wall. His sword was losing its grip. He had to be over halfway down by now.

Rocks pushed the blade out farther. He was about to lose it when he spun around again, holding onto the blade with one hand. He was now basically falling.

Dust and rocks flew in his face, blinding him. The blade came free, and he jumped away from the wall and fell.

He let go of the sword so that he wouldn't land on it. His feet hit the ground first. He tried to bend his knees and roll into a landing like he usually did in similar situations, but this time, he felt a sharp pain in his ankle and rolled to a stop.

He hurt all over. Looking up, he squinted into the sun.

The loud drone buzzed over the edge of the wall where he was standing only a few seconds ago.

Sid let out a mechanical growl, telling Bless to get up.

"Yeah, I hear it." He stood and winced when his full weight hit his ankle. He brushed the dust off his face and shielded the sun from his eyes with his arms.

"Resident. You are under arrest by the New Federation. Do not resist." A loud computer voice boomed from the Drone.

"Seriously?" Bless broke out laughing. He couldn't run if he wanted to now with a hurt leg. He didn't know how bad it was, but it wasn't good, that was for sure.

"Resident. Do not move. Standby for containment," the drone shouted again. The sound that blasted from its speakers was deafening.

Sid walked up and let out a mechanical bark at the Drone.

"Yeah, you tell him, Sid." Bless looked into the sun.

The drone was a transport container model, the same size as the one he and Citizen had just escaped from. It hovered lower, and the bay doors creaked open.

As it came closer to him, he saw the nano-gun extend out and move to aim.

"Dammit," he whispered, then shook his head.

The drone was lower than the cliff now, by a good ten feet. But it was way too far away from the cliff for someone to make that jump.

Was she going to save him? Where was Citizen?

The drone slowed, and the nano-gun powered up and locked onto Bless.

"Resident. Do not move. Standby for containment," it repeated, twenty feet lower.

"What, do I look like I'm resisting?" Bless raised his arms in submission, ready to get hit with the nano-cables again. He winced, dreading the impact.

A shadow moved across the ground. It was Citizen.

She leaped from the cliff. Her legs stretched out

as if she was running through the air. Both arms extended with her daggers in hand. Her body slammed into the side of the drone, knocking it off course just as it shot.

The nano-cable sailed past Bless. He dove to the ground and rolled out of the way.

Citizen had stuck her daggers into the side of the metal container and was hanging on by the handles.

"What took you so long?" Bless dusted off his pants.

"Me? You took forever to get down the hill." Her extra weight made the drone dip and spin.

The nano-gun was pointing in all directions, and the drone's engines strained against the weight of Citizen's body. It spun around.

"Be careful." He cracked a grin. "You might fall off."

"Really? You don't say?" She climbed to the top and repeatedly stabbed into the control unit on the roof. "Thanks for that sound advice."

"Happy to help." The Drone flew over Julian's head and circled above.

Sparks and smoke shot out from the engine, and it fell to the ground in a crash that shook Julian's teeth.

"Citizen." He yelled her name, his throat raw and parched.

Out of the pile of dust and spinning rotor blades, Citizen launched herself off of the wreck just before it landed.

Flipping in the air, she landed on her feet, tucked her body, rolled into a tight ball, and then stood upright in front of Julian. She wiped her hair out of her eyes with a fist that still held a dagger. In the background behind her, the crashed drone came to a halt.

"You okay?" She held his gaze.

"Yeah." Bless took a step, then winced.

"You're injured?" Worry masked her face.

"Something's wrong with my ankle," said Julian. "Hurt it on the way down. Are you okay?"

"Yes, I'm fine." She reached back to sheath her daggers.

Sid walked up, holding Julian's katana in his mouth. Julian took the sword and secured it back on his belt.

"The rest of that Federation squad isn't far behind," said Citizen. "We have to . . ."

She took a step forward, flinched, and then tripped, landing on the soft dirt.

Julian limped toward her. "Are you sure you're all right?"

Citizen shook her head. "D-don't know." Her eyes looked dazed. "M-my vestibular system shows an error." She grabbed her head at the temples. "Running d-diagnostics. It looks like I took a high voltage shock when I smashed t-that turbine. One nerve synapse has blown. I'm okay, j-just gonna be a little slow until I can reboot."

Julian eyed her with worry, then helped her to her feet. "Let's get started moving then."

9

Octavian Karr

Commander Karr sat in his office. He leaned forward on the metal desk and steepled his fingers in front of him. Handler Nev Meechum stood before him, holding a datapad. "Tell me again what happened?"

"According to the log . . ." Meechum slid her finger over the device. "Let's see. Drone 0313 lost signal at 1537, in sector fifty-two right on course on its return flight." She pushed bangs out of her face.

"And it contained the two suspects at that time?" Commander Karr felt the anger rising inside him.

"Yes, Sir," said Meechum. "They were both successfully restrained. All of that is on the video feed. We know now that the drone hit the dome wall first. It obviously couldn't get through. It re-sent a request for new coordinates, but when it didn't receive any, it landed."

"Why did the shield come up before the drone was inside?" He clenched his teeth so hard, his jaws ached.

"Don't know, Sir. The best I have on that is the timing remained off on the drone fleet. Since the shield wall had never gone up, it didn't take as long as the expected sixteen and a half minutes. All walls were fully up in just over fourteen minutes."

"So, an administrative foul-up? Is that what cost me my fugitives?"

"Yes, Sir. It's not as if anyone had tested the Doomsday Protocol before."

"And what of the scouting party deployed from Outpost Nine?"

"They arrived at the crash site roughly three minutes after the drone went down." She spun the datapad around to show him and scrolled through the images. "It appears something attacked it from the outside, damaged the housing unit, and tore out the control board here." She pointed to the last photo.

"And the team followed the two fugitives?"

"That's right, Sir."

"Have they reported in?"

"Not yet, Sir," replied Meechum. "Their check-in is in about ten minutes."

"Update me as soon as you hear from them," he said. "What does your field experience tell you, Handler Meechum? Is that the work of a 2.0?"

Meechum looked at the photo again and enlarged the image with her fingers. "I don't know, Sir. It looks like the metal was hit and damaged with tools. It looks like metal on metal. I don't think a Gollum, even a 2.0, would do that. They're not known to use tools of any kind."

Commander Karr nodded in agreement. "Maybe someone from the outside smashed the drone and saved them?" If so, he wanted a line on whoever helped them.

Meechum shrugged. "Could be. But the drone didn't pick up any life forms nearby. And transmitted packets of data didn't show any. We just don't know, Sir."

"What do *we* know?" He would learn nothing new from this report. Hopefully, the soldiers on the ground would have more intel. "And we have no other drones available?"

"Not yet, Sir. The only drone in that sector is with the squad. The next available drone is at Base Five, about twenty-four miles away."

He sighed. "All right, call me when the squad reports in."

"Will do, Sir." Meechum turned on her heels and walked out.

Damn. What was going on now? If Drayson had only listened to him and not ordered the lockdown so quickly, Bless, and the Sythy would be in hand now.

Damnable counsel that Drayson had drummed up came back to bite them. He shook his head. *Representative Bachus is a political enemy and is indeed listing the mission failures to the doctor even now.*

Commander Karr liked the system they had before Drayson formed the Top Counsel. He walked into his office and closed the door.

Some top counsel. He slammed his fist on the desk.

It was supposed to be a strategic group that shared intel on the highest levels. An attempt to get the agencies talking together and overall act quicker. But like all things Representative Bachus infected, it had turned into a babbling mess of too many heads in one room. All members were rarely available simultaneously and seldom when an emergency call came through.

Things moved much quicker the old way. It wouldn't have surprised Karr if the entire council itself was Representative Bachus' idea. A way for him to slither up the chain of command. He was just a mere Representative, anyway.

He respected Dr. Drayson like always, but he couldn't put together what the older man was thinking lately. The group either rushed decisions through without thinking or made him wait for the approval. They even sped the Doomsday Protocol through. Now, New Therian was in lockdown for two weeks. It may have stopped the 2.0 attack on the city, but it cost the mission.

Not only was Julian Bless still at large, but now, he and the council were dealing with a rogue Syth-L.

CH012 would know about the attempt to capture her, and if she was free, it was unlikely she would be happy about it. But she should still have a drive to complete her mission. A Syth-L could not break mission protocol without permission. But there was no telling what she would do. They both needed to be captured and quick. He would not tell. Dr. Drayson that he had lost one of the most sophisticated and expensive pieces of Federation technology.

"Commander Karr." His commlink sparked.

Karr hit the button on his shoulder. "Karr, here." He started walking to the door. He knew it was Meechum.

"Squad Three is reporting in," she said.

"I'm on my way." Karr left the office and speed-walked down the grated metal hallway. He took the stairs since they would be faster than the lift. He came into Meechum's special control room and walked up to the console where she had the video link pulled up.

"Commander Karr is here, Sergeant," said Meechum.

"Sir," the Sergeant looked into the screen. "I just sent the video of the second crash site."

"Second crash site?" Karr leaned in for a closer look.

"Yes, Sir. It looks like they took down the second drone, as well. This time, next to a river." Karr watched the video, examining another downed drone from one of the soldier's helmet cams.

"We've retrieved the data card and will upload its contents. But won't be able to make a full transfer until we get back to base."

Damn shield wall. This is going to slow everything down.

How did Drayson expect him to conduct missions with the entire city shielded, blocking any transmissions? The only way they could speak to the Sergeant now was via satellite relay. "What of the two fugitives?"

"Nothing but tracks, Sir. We'll follow them. We can't be too far behind. But there is something else."

"What?" At this point, Karr wasn't sure he wanted to know unless it was news that moved the mission forward and on track.

"There's another set of tracks," said the Sergeant. "A third set. And we're not certain, but it looks like the tracks of a canine-bot."

"What?" Karr had a desire to hit something but refrained for now. He'd take it out in the boxing ring later. "With them?"

"Looks that way, Sir."

"Has there ever been a Federation bot that has had its code broken?" Karr thought back to classified reports on Bless'.

"No, Sir, not that I know of. I'm just telling you what it looks like," the Sergeant said. "No one has the tech out here to power anything close to a bot. But we'll keep moving. I'll report in at the next window."

"Outstanding, Sergeant," said Karr.

"Squad Three out." The video shut off.

"How are their vitals?" Karr asked.

Handler Meechum touched more buttons on the screen. Eight individual photos of the soldiers popped up on the screen—each with a list of vitals and EKG graphs displayed next to them. Three of them flashed in the red. "Five of the eight have not yet reached their VO2 max, including Sergeant Shef-fel. But with the shield wall up, remember, any data is going through satellite relay, so we have about a sixty-second delay."

"Good," said Karr. "Keep them going. I want those two caught immediately."

"Yes, Sir." Meechum touched the screen, bringing it to life, and Karr walked out.

JULIAN BLESS

Julian limped along with Citizen. Both were supporting each other.

His ankle was on fire. He dared not take his boot off. If he did, he'd never get it back on.

Lucky for him, Citizen could support his weight and hers, but her legs twitched every fifth or sixth step. But even with the delay, they had made it to his goal, a rundown bunker, before the next wave of Federation scouts had come upon them.

The riverbed they had been following now widened out into a massive flatland. Bless was way north of where he and Citizen had started.

"Citizen," said Julian. "How far have we gone?"

"Four point two miles since we left the crash site." Citizen helped lower him down to sit on the concrete bunker wall. "And only twenty minutes since the last time you asked that same question, Snowball."

Sid trotted around the structure, scanning for anything of use.

"My sensors say the Federation Squad is about ten minutes behind us, but they're picking up speed."

Her feet twitched again, and she stumbled but caught herself. She sat down too.

"Will the twitching improve like your speech?"

"No, Snowball." She emphasized the pet name, then shook her head. "I rerouted pathways to ensure uninterrupted speech. But I will need to reboot to correct the other issues."

Citizen had saved his life more than once today. And there had been a change in her. What it was exactly, he couldn't put his finger on it. She was still mysterious and had no emotion chip as far as he could tell.

He didn't know what she would have to do for him to trust her. Maybe a man couldn't trust a Sythy completely? But somehow, this one was different.

"Looks like neither one of us are speeding up anytime soon." Julian rubbed his leg.

"Our odds are greater if we defend here." Citizen looked around. "We must fight."

"They'll have pulse rifles, though, right?"

"That is standard squadron equipment."

"Do you know how many there are for sure?"

"Can't tell yet," said Citizen. "They have to be in range to confirm. I'll know in two minutes." She paused a moment as if in thought. "The dura-glass shield wall that is around the city will prevent instant communication. This will slow them down."

"How so?"

"They'll have to relay all traffic through a satellite. And they won't be able to send reinforcements from inside. So, the only Federation troops that will put us in danger are the ones already stationed at the satellite posts before the activation of the wall."

"How long will the wall stay up?"

"It's more of a dome," said Citizen. "It will remain up for fourteen days."

"So, why are you running with me? Weren't you programmed with a mission to arrest and capture me? I thought you couldn't go against your programming?"

Not that he was complaining, but he still found her mysterious, a curiosity of sorts.

Citizen's golden-yellow eyes stared into his. She squinted like she was reading every line in his face.

"Yes, we still have programming, but it's not the same as the old version fives. They allow us to make our own choices."

What? That made little sense. "You mean you can make choices within the CPU's parameters, right?" Her use of the word 'we' stood out.

"I have to complete my mission, but I decide how I do it."

Bless didn't believe her. "So, you still have to bring me to New Therian headquarters? That's your mission, right?"

"Yes, but it's more complicated than that."

"If you can't override your mission, how is that a choice?"

Citizen looked at him as if stuck.

"I make all kinds of choices, Snowball," said Citizen. "I chose to save you by destroying that drone. I chose to jump. I chose everything."

"Yes, but you still have to complete your mission, correct?"

"That's right."

"Their new program gives you the illusion of choice." Bless inspected his swollen ankle and winced. "You get to make choices, but your programming still forces you within the parameters of the mission. You only have the illusion of choice."

Citizen looked off into the distance where the

squad was coming from. "There are eight individuals and one canine. A real canine, not a bot. What if I reprogram my mission?"

"Can you do that?"

"Yes, but only with approval from a mission handler, or someone who can override mission protocol, like a battalion commander or higher."

Julian shook his head. "I see. You may be more like us than I thought. That is why in Elysium, we have free will. Elysium is not bound to the rules or fate of the Federation. We live free out here, just as everyone should be. Just as you should."

"You have the information about the virus and the Trolls." Citizen held his gaze. "The people need to hear it. And they need to hear it from you since you were part of the original team. We have to get you inside the city to get your message out."

"How are you going to do that while still completing your mission?"

"I will have to find a way to override mission protocol."

Citizen stared at him again, taking in the information. Then her legs jerked, and her shoulders hunched over for a split second. She winced in pain. "I need rebooting soon. They will be here in three minutes. She stood up and pulled out both daggers."

Sid walked up to them. A growl noise echoed from his speaker.

Bless drew his sword. "My Kendo teacher always told me never to bring a blade to a fight of pulse rifles."

Citizen nodded. "That is wise. But not always correct." She stood on the broken concrete wall. "You stay here in this corner, with your back to the wall. They will not see you until they get past me." She pointed forward. "Sid, you remain on that side. If we attack from both directions, we have a high chance of success." The bot move over to where Citizen pointed.

"Even with the pulse rifles?" Julian used the wall to stand up.

"Yes. Ah." Citizen shouted a brief cry of pain. Her legs and arm twitched, and she dropped the dagger from that arm. "Our chances just lowered by ten percent." She bent down to pick up the dagger.

"Wow, that makes all the difference in the world." Julian leaned against the concrete and wrapped both hands around the grip, warming it up. "Thanks for sharing."

"One minute," said Citizen.

A dog barked, and a man's voice filtered in on the dry breeze.

In front of Bless was the river and a small string

of trees. From his position, he watched Citizen moved to the left, taking cover for the ambush.

Seconds later, a couple of armed Federation soldiers came over the ridge, and a German Shepherd ran towards Bless.

Sid went after the dog, and Citizen ran toward the two men.

Shots fired from pulse rifles, and more soldiers came into view.

Then out of the tree line came another group of people flanking the soldiers. That seemed to surprise the Feds, and it divided their attention. The group that attacked were Elysium. They had swords and staffs and engaged in close combat.

Sid took care of the dog and ran after the next closest soldier.

Citizen had already killed one. Then a pulse rifle shot hit her, and she went down.

One soldier ran towards Bless, but he didn't have a pulse rifle. Instead, the Fed had a pistol.

Bless ducked behind the concrete and crawled forward. Bullets hit above him.

He raised his Katana, then inched closer to the soldier.

The Fed pointed the gun at Bless' chest, making his heart pound against his ribs.

Captured by a female Sythy, hunted by the Federation, and two crashes under his belt, were about all he was willing to take today.

"Go ahead. Pull the trigger." Bless held the Fed's stone-hard gaze. "Because if you don't, I'm going to—"

A dagger flew through the air, lodging itself in the man's forearm. The Fed dropped the gun and grabbed his knife.

Bless ran and limped up as fast as he could. With the reach of his sword, are extended, he closed the gap. Julian sliced the hand and then, with a back-swing, cut the soldier across the neck.

Citizen stood over her last kill, twitching.

Sid and three Elysium stood before Bless, with eight dead Federation soldiers.

A glance confirmed the dead and wounded were mainly Federation, and then there was Citizen, who had a bullet hole in her arm. It wasn't fatal, but it would need attention. She twitched again, then stumbled.

Two of the dead Elysium, who had come out of nowhere prior, were shot by high-powered pulse rifles, which Bless now confiscated.

Footsteps sounded behind him, and he turned to see a familiar face.

"Brother Bless." Hector pushed his dirty shemagh

off his head, revealing a mess of blonde hair and a beard. He raised two muscular arms that clasped around Bless, then hugged him.

"Hector, you have good timing, my friend." Julian patted him on the back.

"Are you all right?" Hector eyed him with concern.

"Yes, I'm fine. How are our people?"

Dak, the large man more prominent than two of Julian, stood, surveying the battlefield.

"The rest are dead." Tella picked up a pulse rifle and checked the load count. "I'll gather the weapons and inventory the ammo."

"Thank you, Tella," said Bless. "Dak, Hector, great to see you. How did you find us?"

"We've been following you since we lost you back fighting the Gollums," said Hector.

Julian shook hands with Dak and hugged Tella.

"Kim and Dev are dead," reported Hector.

"I'm sorry," Bless closed his eyes and shook his head. Losing men was always challenging, and it never got easier.

"Once the Feds know their team is dead, they'll send the next closest team. That's protocol," Citizen's leg twitched, and the hole in her arm smoked.

Hector's eyes widened. "Are you a—"

"A Syth-L, yes." Julian rose and approached her. "She's saved my life twice already. She's with us."

Hector, Dak, and Tella all eyed her skeptically.

Once she could stand again, Citizen began searching the dead Federation soldiers next to her. Tella did the same. Citizen stripped a med-pack off the body, and she carried it to Bless.

"Sit down, Snowball," she said to Bless. "Let me look at your leg."

Bless sat and pulled up his pant leg. Citizen untied the laces, pulled off his boot, then opened the soldier's med-pack.

She rested the leg on her knee and pulled out a Bone Scanner that was the size of a large pen. Clicking it on, a flat blue beam of light shot out. She held it steady and moved it over his swollen ankle. It beeped, and she looked at the display.

"Well, what's it say?" Bless stared at the device.

"You broke nothing. It's just a sprain. Painful, but you'll be all right." She grabbed a Morphin-asol syringe and stabbed that into the wound.

"A bit of a warning next time would be good before you stab me." Bless didn't flinch. But he felt the pain go away immediately.

"It'll last at least twenty-four hours." Citizen rummaged through the med-pack.

Next came the Stem Cell syringe, and she injected that too without warning. Lastly, she ripped apart a plastic bag that contained a Nano Brace. She laid the black nano-sheet over the swollen ankle and hit the activation button on the remote, and the nano-tech sheet formed and molded over his wounded ankle.

"Put it on." She shoved his boot against his chest.

"Yes, Ma'am." Bless forced his boot on, then laced it as tight as he could.

"It isn't too tight, is it?" Citizen examined his work. "Okay, you're good to go." She patted his leg. "Let's move."

"Thanks." Julian groaned, then stood up. The pain was already going away, and the nano-brace flexed and provided support as he walked.

Hector, Dak, and Tella walked up. They had all stripped the soldiers of weapons, med-packs, nutrient tubes, and hydro packs.

"Me and a handful of others came to look for you after the Gollum attack," said Hector. "It took us a while, but here we are."

"Where's the rest of the group?" Bless looked around.

"Probably ten miles south by now," said Tella. "They're trying to evac people out of the path of the

Gollum herd. We can meet up with them if we head out now."

"The next Federation Squad will come from that direction." Citizen dropped the syringe of stem cells she had just injected into her arm, then wrapped a bandage around the wound. Then her legs twitched, nearly falling off of her perch.

"What the hell is wrong with you?" Tella asked her.

"Electrical shock to my synapses, I need a power reboot. But I must find a source of at least twenty megawatts for that."

Hector looked at Dak and Tella. "What about Chimney Base?"

Dak nodded, then grunted.

"We haven't been there for over a year," said Julian. "Is it still deserted?"

"Should be," said Hector.

"Chimney Base would have a power cell that big," said Tella. "But we need a late version connection to turn it on."

"I can provide that," said Citizen. "How far is it?"

"Two days by foot, northwest," said Hector.

Another Fed squad was coming. No time to bury the dead. Bless wasn't a hundred percent, and neither was Citizen. And they were a long way from help.

What is the best call? He rubbed his temples.

"I say we head for Chimney Base," said Bless. "We need her. Citizen can take out Gollums, soldiers, and even a drone single-handedly."

"We'll follow you, Brother Bless," said Hector. "Lead the way."

Octavian Karr

Commander Karr stood by the control terminal once again. "You mean to tell me that Bless and one Syth-L took out a full drone and an entire eight-man squad?"

"That's what it looks like, Sir," said Handler Meechum. "Remember, her combat readiness is at a Tier One level. It's not outside her capabilities. And they appear to have a canine bot with them."

"Damn. Activate Team Five," said Karr. "I want them stopped. How far out are they?"

Meechum typed. "Team Five can reach them in approximately sixteen hours."

"Good. Send them. And activate Team Six as well."

"Sending the file now."

"I need your terminal," said Commander Karr. "Please cease."

"Yes, Sir." Meechum got up and left, closing the door behind her.

Commander Karr sat down on the swivel chair and brought up the navigation screen. He went to settings, control panel, and then to administrator login. He put in his code. The screen flashed, then reset. In the search bar, he typed 'CH012SYTH-L.' He needed to know more, but he couldn't trust a mere handler.

A picture of the Syth-L and several headings came up.

"Let's see who this Sythy is, who now causes so many problems."

He touched the link that read 'File History' and scrolled through, reading as much pertinent information as he could find—born in the Human Study Group AA16. Parents were from Operation Blue Thunder, both unwilling participants. *Nothing unusual there.* They were disciplined and arrested for insubordination multiple times, eventually sent to Camp Trenton for reassignment.

Genetic Enhancements Delta, Kilo, Lima,

November, and X-ray were all a hundred percent effective at birth. Age twelve, Bravo, Charlie, Romeo, Sierra, and Yankee are only seventy-five percent effective. She passed primary training at the top of her class. No record of her body rejecting any allografts or implants. Sent to Citizen Hill facility at age sixteen. No recorded anomalies.

Hmmm. You are an interesting girl, aren't you?

He tapped a few other links. *Nothing unusual popped up.* So, he went back and clicked on Study Group AA16.

He scrolled down the lists of batches and years. Operation Blue Thunder was highlighted in red.

He hovered over it. Then he decided against going back there.

Lab 7 was highlighted orange. *Interesting.* He clicked on it. Her biological parents were unwilling participants back in the early days of the New Federation. He clicked on the father. No infractions. He clicked on the mother, Resident 0773648.

A list of violations highlighted in orange filled the screen.

Holy shit. The mother was quite the rebel back in the early days.

Local, District, and Federal violations. Multiple reassignment times. Terrorist watch list. Associated with the group Yellow Dawn. Five different Enemy of the State labels.

Karr sat back. He was aware of some anomalies that plagued the early experiments, but much had changed since then. He had to talk to a *special* someone to find out more. And *he* was the one person in the Federation that Karr despised. Representative Bachus.

He backed out of the screen, signed off. The screen went back to black.

CITIZEN HILL

Citizen Hill woke up. It was still dark, and everyone else was still sleeping. Other than Dak, who stood guard sitting up against a rock about thirty yards away. She didn't have to sleep as much as a fleshy, but the human parts in repair still needed rest. Even more so now, after her electrical injury. The bullet hole in her arm was no longer an issue. She just had to keep it covered to prevent infection.

She stood, and her legs twitched. *Damn. I need a re-set bad.* She looked in her pack. Only half a hydro pack remained. So, she left it alone. She would need it later.

Sid trotted up. His gears spun and whizzed as the bot sat. A whining noise came from his speaker.

"Well, good morning to you too." She smiled and reached out to pat its metal head like she had seen Bless do multiple times.

Funny how they could design a machine that not only acted like a real dog but brought out human emotions from the other fleshys.

"We should get moving," Bless said behind her. He was sitting up and rubbed his bare arms from the cold of the night.

"How is it?" Citizen pointed to his leg.

"Much better, but the pain killer is wearing off." He waved at Dak.

Dak returned a chin lift in recognition. She didn't think she had heard the large man speak a single word since they had been traveling together.

Sid sprung to Bless' side, and Bless used the bot's sturdy metal body to stand up.

"Hey, Hector, Tella," shouted Bless, "rise and shine, children."

Two minutes later, she and Bless and the rest of the group walked northwest in a single file.

Sid scouted out front, and Citizen brought up the rear.

Hours later, the rocky terrain eventually turned into dry, sparse landscapes. What little greenery grew was strangled out by the dense forests. The sun beat down, slowing the progression.

Her uncovered sleeves were allowing her skin to get sunburned. But that was the least of her worries. She knew her handler would have sent the next closest Federation Squad after them by now. They would have to hurry if they wanted to reach Chimney Base by this afternoon.

Bless and the rest of the humans finally stopped to drink the last of their hydro packs.

Hector pushed down his shemagh and wiped the sweat off his face. "How far away do you think our nearest pursuers are?"

"I estimate five to six hours." Citizen perched on a rock at the highest point overlooking the ground they covered and the path before them. "Faster if they have a drone. But not all reaction squads have them. They would move on foot. They're not designed to cover distance like this. But the Federation would have no other forces outside the dome." The sudden jerk of her leg stopped her speech, forcing her to regain her balance or topple.

Bless sipped on his hydro pack. "When was the last time any of us were at Chimney Base?"

"I think Master Dunlam left there with the last team." Tella sat her newly gained pulse rifle down. The short, skinny human was a lot tougher than she looked. "That had to be about a year ago." She kept her weary eyes on Citizen.

Bless took one more sip, then passed the hydro pack to Tella. "What about the others? After the Gollum attack?"

"We lost eleven of us after that one." Hector scratched, then wiped his beard. "We didn't know you were gone until much later. We got spread thin. A few of the Gollum survived, and they took off before we could kill the last of them. Three scout teams went out to find you. Don't know where the other two are."

"So, the main group is pretty small by now?" Bless examined the laces of his boot.

"Yes, Master Dunlam took charge," said Hector. "They were still in pursuit of the herd. They think the horde will move south."

"The shield dome will protect the city," said Citizen, "but it's an automatic death sentence to any of the small outskirt villages right outside." She could tell by the expressions on Hector and Tella. They didn't fully trust her.

"What do you think the Feds are going to do?" Bless shot a glance her way.

"They've got twelve more days before the dome comes down." Citizen held his green, piercing gaze. "They don't have enough of a force to fight the

Gollums out here." Her legs jerked. "Protocol would advise to combine battalions and meeting the herd at the border right when the dome goes down."

"How will they know where the herd will be at that moment?" Hector used a torn cloth of fabric to wipe off his arms.

"I don't think they will. They'll have to get eyes outside," said Citizen. "But until then, nothing goes in or out of the main—"

An incoming transmission signal popped up on her GUI vision, and she looked down to concentrate.

"What is it?" Bless rose, then approached her.

"A handler is requesting transmission," she said. "It's on a sixty-second delay. We can't send any files or codes, just text."

"What are they saying?" Hector faced her, suspicion burning in his eyes.

"I can only read the subject line. The dispatch is labeled 'Request Check-in.' They know I've gone rogue, but they don't know my location. If I open the transmission text, they'll get a ping on my coordinates. So, I can't open it."

Sid popped up from the top of a hill and let out a loud bark from his speaker.

"Break is over." Bless motioned for everyone to stand.

Together, the group began walking again and followed Sid's tracks into the blazing sun. Hours passed.

The pain in her nerves was excruciating. It got worse with every step. To be used to the cybernetic implants for so many years, she forgot how badly it hurt when something went wrong. The pain that emitted from her human nerves reminded her of what it must feel like to be a human and to deal with pain all the time.

She glanced at Bless. How much pain does he feel in his ankle each time he takes a step?

Both knees locked up for a split second with another twitch. Pain shot through her legs. She would think twice before sinking her metal blade into a large drone capacitor again. She was lucky the synapses just needed rebooting, and nothing was fried. But one blank synapse passed the signal to the next, causing an overload to the next link in the chain. Then that synapse would fail. Her central nervous system would continue to get more overloaded the longer she went without a reboot.

Pain. What a normal human experience.

It was one of those rare sensations or feelings she understood in a similar way to a fleshy. Her nerves, circulatory, respiration, and much of her endocrine system, were some of the physiological traits that she knew were still fully human. They were enhanced but were not synthetic. Therefore, they were her weakest points, but they were the ones that connected her to humanity. They were the connecting points between her original biological body and her synthetic parts.

She didn't like the pain, but it reminded her of some humanity deep within. Some urge encoded deep within her tiniest cells. She didn't know what it was, but she knew it was real and alive.

"Here it is." Hector came to a full stop.

Sid trotted up, and the group walked around an enormous iron door that stuck out from the ground. Dak and Tella began kicking away dirt and removing rocks. Sid dug, assisting with his front paws.

Citizen and Hector moved to the locking mechanism.

"I got this." Hector pulled a pick tool from a slot in his backpack, scraped dirt out of the keyhole, and then blew on it to blast out the remaining dust.

He jammed the pick into the lock and hit the activation button on the end.

The pick buzzed, then the light turned from red to green. A clang rung under the door and the metal locks squeaked open.

Dak and Bless grabbed one of the enormous

doors and pulled it open, revealing a dusty metal staircase. They went down.

Citizen's leg twitched on the second stair, and she almost stumbled, but she was able to hold on to the railing.

When they reached the ground floor, they switched on their high beam flashlights.

Citizen switched to night vision.

"All right," said Bless. "Dak and Tella, you search the barracks for any food or water. Hector, you watch the door. I'll help Citizen with the reboot."

Sid followed Bless and Citizen. It didn't take Bless long to find the main control room. Once inside the chamber, Citizen walked up to the control console.

A thick layer of dust covered everything.

"It's dead." Citizen let out a long sigh. "This is old tech."

"Yeah." Bless toyed with a panel, pulling it loose. "But it'll work as long as the power cells weren't completely dry."

She found another panel and brushed off as much dust as she could. She opened it to reveal several different ports. It would most likely have a Version Seven Port. That is all she would need. There it was. She unwrapped her bandaged arm and pulled out a dagger.

On the underside of her forearm, she took the point of the blade and slowly dug it up, making a slit out of the bullet hole. Pain again. But it barely registered this time.

She dug in with her fingers and pulled out the auxiliary jack.

Good thing the shot didn't land three inches higher. The cord unfolded about a foot long.

She bit the plastic cap with her teeth, pulled it off, and then plugged it into the port.

The distinct coppery tang of blood coated her mouth.

Bless dragged an old chair next to her. "Sit down."

A tiny power icon blinked in her GUI vision. After a couple of minutes of silence, the icon came to life.

External device detected: it read.

Citizen began the power transfer—lines of code scrolled through her vision.

Device startup. Yes or No: it read at the bottom.

"Yes," she said barely above a whisper.

Bless continued to examine the other open panel.

"Careful what you touch over there, Snowball," said Citizen. "You could run into a hot wire."

Lights began blinking across the console. The flat touch screen turned from black to light gray.

"I'll take that under advisement." Bless returned the plate panel, then leaned against the console.

Citizen wiped away a thick layer of dust from the screen, trying to free up the touch surface.

The touch screen blinked, turned white, then an old Federation logo materialized in the center.

Citizen touched the home screen with her free hand and began picking her way through the task list. Sometimes, she had to press the screen two or three times for the command to take, but it was working.

Settings. Tap.

Network. Tap. Tap.

Updates and Applications. Tap. Tap. Tap with more force.

Power. Tap.

A graphic readout of eight different power cells and two solar inputs appeared—the two solars were at zero percent. Three power cells were at zero percent, as well. One read 'critical' nine percent in red, and the last two read 'low' at twenty-five and twenty-two percent, respectively. That would be enough.

She tapped the twenty-five percent, and it enlarged on the screen.

Control Panel. Tap.

Power Output Transfer. Tap. Tap.

A box popped up and read: *security authentication required.*

She typed in the Federation Administrative code.

Begin Transfer. Tap.

The power cell icon blinked.

"Is it working?" Bless looked on. Curiosity masked his face.

"Yes, it'll take a few minutes." Citizen sat back in the chair. Her legs jerked, and her knees straightened, making her feet kick the console.

"Damn, that hurt." She avoided his probing gaze.

A long progress bar appeared in her GUI: 0%, 2%, 4%, the bar slowly grew

Incoming message from the handler.

Request check-in: the message title read.

They were still trying. She would not bite, especially now that she was this close.

It's safe to answer: the next message title said.

Yeah, right. A dry laugh escaped her lips.

They know U R at old base B79: the next one read.

What? That's the ID number of this location.

Then she saw on the screen: *Fed Team 5 is 1 hour away.*

What the hell? Is the handler relaying information? Was it a trap? Or is she helping?

It must be a trap. They would not trick her. But how did they know she was here at this exact base?

There was no way that turning on this old console connected them to the city grid.

"You doing okay over there?" Bless crossed his legs, taking weight off his injured ankle.

"Yes. Perhaps you should sit and elevate your leg." She adjusted the line attached to her arm. "This could take a while."

The progress bar flashed: *12%, 14% . . .*

I know you won't answer: the message title read, then the connection buffered as if another message was loading. *Trust me. Search Project Blue Thunder in location records*

Something was wrong. She wanted to answer the handler but knew she couldn't. But if the Feds knew her location anyway, what did it matter?

She minimized the power cell screen and tapped on the home screen.

Location Records. Tap.

Search. Tap. Tap.

Security Authentication Required popped up on the screen.

She typed in the admin code she used before.

Security denied. The box restarted, then flashed a few times. *Use code 917263gDa969QjG234rj77hd743.*

Sitting back, she stared at the screen.

How the hell does the handler know what's going on?

The power bar kept growing: *32%, 34% . . .*

What would happen if she put in that code? What was Operation Blue Thunder? Who was talking to her?

"Everything all right?" Bless pulled up a wooden box and sat. Then he retrieved a med-pack.

"Yes, fine." She continued to focus on the readout screen. "Almost at fifty percent. Just a few more minutes."

Citizen had a choice. But she couldn't calculate the risk because she had no reference points to input. She typed in the code, hovered over the screen for a second, then tapped.

A list of files appeared.

So, the code does work. A surge of energy shot through her body, but she wasn't sure if the buzz was from the impending reboot, the synapse misfires, or the need to know what was going on.

She typed 'Operation Blue Thunder' and hit search.

Eighteen documents labeled Operation Blue Thunder 1-18 appeared.

Download Files. Tap.

Download complete.

She knew she wouldn't have time to read it all here. She would take them with her.

The bar read: *56%, 58% . . .*

Citizen went back to the search screen. *What did that code do? What else could it find?*

She hit the search field again, then put in the long code from before.

Her fingers hovered over the screen. Then she typed 'Syth-L program enhancements' in and hit search.

Updates. Tap.

Physical and Biological. Tap.

Possible Enhancements. Tap.

Cellular? No.

Microbiological? No.

Emotional. Tap

"What are you doing?" Bless finished injecting the last Morphin-asol syringe into his ankle.

"Nothing, just finishing the transfer."

System Upgrades Available. Tap.

A long list of emotion package chips blinked on the screen. She scrolled to the bottom. Emotion Package XY BETA was the latest design.

The publication date was only twenty-seven days ago. This chip was the newest one, and it was still in beta phase.

She tapped on it: *Restricted Access. Manual Access Only. Building 44R.*

That made sense. It wouldn't be online if it were still in beta testing. But she could get it if she could get inside Building 44R. But that was in the capital district, inside headquarters.

What would that new chip do?

She went back to the search field and typed 'Project Goldfish' that Bless had mentioned earlier. Twenty-six files appeared. She downloaded them as well.

The bar continued to make progress: *96%, 98%, 100%.*

A message popped up. *Request restart. Yes or No.*

"Yes," she said.

Primary Physio-Control: read on the screen. Yes or No.

"Yes." Her entire body convulsed, and her muscles flexed. She gritted her teeth, and a white-hot pain shot through her body.

"Are you okay?" Bless stepped toward her, then kneeled.

The pain passed as quickly as it came. "Yeah, I'm fine."

Citizen flexed her fingers and rolled her head from side to side. The synapses were flowing again. She stood, powered down the console, unplugged the wire, tucked it back in her forearm, then re-bandaged the wound.

Team 5 approaches from the east. Get moving: the next subject line from the handler scrolled past.

Who was this? Could she risk sending a message? If they knew her position already, what would it matter? She mused over the same question she posed earlier. The handler had to know because she identified the base number. She had to know the risk.

Who R U? What is your ID number?: Citizen put in the subject line and sent it.

"Okay, you all good?" Bless rose, but he continued to stand over her.

"Yes, let's get out of here."

Call me Sunflower: the handler replied.

Sunflower? Handlers only used ID numbers. This was some codename. *What the hell?*

A burst of pulse rifle fire erupted through the steel walls.

"Bless, we got company," yelled Tella.

Citizen and Bless ran toward the door.

More pulse rifle fire. The sound echoed. Then more fire.

Citizen pulled a dagger and ran to the source location.

Both Tella and Dak were backing up from the hall, firing into the room they were backing away from.

"What's going on?" Hector yelled from the stairs.

"A whole barracks full of scabbies and Gollums," yelled Tella. "Let's get out of this death box."

Sid was the first up the stairs, Bless and Citizen right behind him. Tella and Dak brought up the rear, backing up the stairs, still firing a shot here or there. Everyone got up to the main level. Citizen lifted the metal door, and once everyone was out, she dropped it in place, then waited for it to lock down snugly. When the light flashed from green to red, she released the handle.

"Whew," said Tella. "Bad news, we didn't find any food. Good news, we didn't get eaten by that horde." She pulled out the battery pack on her rifle and checked the counter.

"Were they Trolls or regular?" Bless surveyed the area.

"Regular." Tella shouldered the rifle.

"We need to move west." Citizen headed out.

"Why west?" Hector adjusted the pack on his back.

"Feds are coming from the east." Citizen didn't bother looking back because forward was the only option at this point.

"Let's move." Bless joined her, pacing his stride with hers.

A thought came to her. We're *an odd group.*

She chuckled to herself.

We're a band of four humans, one Sythy, and a canine bot on our way to the wasteland.

13

JULIAN BLESS

It had been another day-and-a-half of fast move-ment. Julian's ankle was feeling much better, but only because of the nano-splint. If he hadn't been walking all day, it might have healed by now with the stem cells. But he had no choice in the matter.

The sun had just gone down, and the small group walked down a valley. Green lush grass grew in the soil-rich earth. An array of wildlife, mainly small vermin of the rodent and marsupial kind, hurried about, here and there, avoid contact.

Citizen was back to her normal hundred percent strength and speed. Sid had been doing the scouting.

And he and the rest of his group had little food and even less rest over the last few days.

Everyone's tired, but they're Elysium. They're used to a challenging pace.

Bless was debating how far he should push the group tonight when Sid ran into view, making barking noises.

Citizen ran up to meet the bot, tapped him on the head, then ran up to the nearest hill.

Does she communicate with the bot? The thought intrigued him.

She came back with a smile on her face. "Looks like we made it."

"Where?" Bless glanced from Citizen to the bot.

"Back to Elysium." Her speech was nonchalant.

Bless, and the others crested the hill and saw the familiar tents and setup of the Elysium camp. The wagons and carts were situated in a circle in the middle. There were multiple campfires scattered around.

Bless was over-joyed at finding his family again. But then his joy turned to pain as soon as he realized why there were so few campfires.

Elysium was a fraction of the size it used to be. *They had lost many over the last few days, and now, many more would perish.*

At camp, Julian sat with his seniors. Master

Dunlam and Master Clark were next to him. Hector sat on the other side of the fire, poking it with a long stick.

"Now that you're back amongst us." Master Dunlam stroked the embers of the fire with a blacken-tipped stick. "Elysium is fifty-seven strong."

Julian rubbed his chin. "We've lost a lot."

"We may be few," said Master Clark, "but everyone is in high spirits today, knowing that *you* are alive. The other two scout teams never returned. We didn't want to give up hope."

Citizen walked up with Tella, who carried a large paper map. One of the old ones that were extremely rare. It was one of the only two that Elysium still had.

"Look here." Tella moved to one of the carts.

Dunlam and Clark rose. Each held a lantern in hand. Bless, and the others cleared off the cart to lay the map down.

"All right." Citizen smoothed the edges of the map. "I just completed my final scan from on top of that ridge. We are here west of New Therian." Her finger pointed to the location. "They completely shut the capital city off from us by raising the dome shield. There's no going in or out for another nine days."

"This is good since no more Federation Troops can attack us from the city," replies Master Clark.

"Yes. But it's equally devastating to the people in the outskirts." Citizen tapped the map. "What do we know of the Troll horde?"

"The large herd, the main one that we fought before, is here." Master Dunlam pointed on the map south of their current position. "They are working their way to the shield dome, attacking everything they find in their path. They're on a course headed straight to the township of Benton." He traced his finger down the map.

"Benton, we've been there before, right?" Hector worked his way into the group, wiggling between Tella and Citizen.

"Yes," said Julian. "We have many supporters there. But they're defenseless."

"The Federation Squad is approaching here." Citizen pointed north of their location. "And I don't know for sure, but I expect they're sending the next closest squad, which would be Squad 6 from here."

"So, it looks like we have two choices," said Master Dunlam said.

"Two?" Bless peered up.

"We either move out west to safety," said Dunlam, "or we move southeast towards Benton, the Troll herd, and the two squads of Feds?"

"That's right." Julian ran a hand through his hair. "But there's no choice. We have to go to Benton to help protect them."

Master Dunlam looked around. "I know Brother Bless. We all want to. But we have so few numbers. Many of Elysium think we should go back to the hills until we're stronger in numbers."

Julian knew the risk. He hated these decisions.

"We have to do what's best for Elysium. And we are all"—Bless circled the entire section of the map that was outside of New Therian—"All, Elysium."

Everyone silently nodded in agreement.

"There is one more thing," said Citizen, her tone low and calm. "We know the dome shield deploys in eight hundred-meter sections. We also know the Federation Army wants the Trolls dead as much as we do."

"Yes, so?" Master Dunlam moved his gaze from the map to focus on her.

Citizen eyed him, then pointed back to the map. "We know the satellite base that the original Federation Squad Four deployed from was this base here." She pointed to a small red dot south of their position. "Hector, Tella, and I came up with this idea."

"Go on." Master Dunlam, now fully engaged, stared, unblinking.

"This satellite base would have a direct hardwired commlink to Federation Headquarters inside the city. They buried the old lines underground. If we hacked the base's main computer, we could tap into the Headquarters' controls and possibly manipulate a section of the shield and lower it." She paused for a second. "Now, if we manage to get only one section of the dome down, that would leave an eight-hundred-meter gap, right here."

"Why would we do that?" Dunlam asked.

"If we create a breach here . . ." Citizen pointed at the wall. "The Troll herd would divert to it. They would merge into a larger population count and head for the city."

"Yes, but—" Julian was digesting the meaning of her words.

"If that happened," Citizen continued, "the bulk of the Federation Army would defend that breach. The populace would be protected, and the most well-armed forces with pulse rifles and drones would be able to fight the herd in a small area. Instead of on an open battlefield where they would surely lose. This would save the innocent people in Benton, eliminate most if not all the Trolls, and give us access to inside New Therian, which was if I'm not mistaken, the mission in the first place."

Bless held his chin. *Damn. That's a good idea.*

"Even if we could reach this base in time," said

Master Dunlam, "how would we be able to break a Federation Code that quick?"

"We have the only person I know of who has already broken a Federation code." She gestured to Bless.

"Okay, if we do manage to break that code." Master Dunlam raised his hands in a questioning posture. "How do you know we'll be able to lower a section of the wall?"

"Because I know." Citizen stared into Master Dunlam's defiance.

"I don't know." Master Dunlam frowned.

"This may work." A newfound surge of hope coursed through his body. "It may work, but we need to think on it some more."

"We've taken some big losses, Brother Bless," Master Dunlam said. "I'm afraid—"

"Of what?" Bless didn't bother hiding his annoyance.

But there was something different about the circle gathered around the map. *What was it?*

Master Dunlam exchanged looks with the two other seniors.

"I'm afraid some decisions were made in your absence." Master Clark joined the conversation.

"What do you mean?" Julian's brows shot up in surprise.

"We all respect you and love you," said Master Dunlam. "And we have followed you for a long time. But Elysium is losing the stomach to continue fighting the Trolls."

"What?" Julian took a step back.

"That's not true." Master Clark raised an arm in the air.

"I'm afraid it is," said Master Dunlam.

"What's going on?" Julian asked.

"Elysium has voted to discontinue the pursuit of the Trolls," said Dunlam.

"That's ridiculous." Julian raised his arms in the air, his frustration visible to all. "If we don't protect the people, less will support us. How is Elysium supposed to grow if we don't have supporters?"

"Master Dunlam has been in charge in your absence. And what he says about the morale is true, but nothing has been decided for sure." Master Clark turned his full attention to Master Dunlam, then said, "We all agreed that we would continue to move south unless we had to move somewhere else for Bless."

"And now we have found him," said Master Dunlam.

"Yes, but now that he is here, we will follow his leadership and get back to our mission," said Master Clark.

Master Dunlam rubbed his wrinkled face, then nodded. "Yes, yes, that is right." He paused a moment. "We are all weary. We are glad you have returned. Elysium is dead without you. It has been a long couple of days. You have eaten, but you're tired from your ordeal. I move that we adjourn for tonight, then discuss plans first thing in the morning."

Bless rubbed his eyes. He felt like he had not slept in days. "Sounds good." But something about the discussion this evening put him on edge.

The group of elders dispersed. Each set off to his respective camp for the evening. Hector remained by Bless.

"I don't like the feeling around here," Hector said in a whisper.

"I know," Bless' eyes narrowed. "I feel it too. Something is off, but I can't place it."

"Something changed while we were gone," said Hector. "It's been five days. We've lost people."

"But it's something more than that," replied Bless. "Did Master Dunlam seem okay to you?"

"I can't tell." Hector grabbed the hair on his chin. "Maybe he's right. We're all burned out. We need rest. We don't know what they've been through. We should just get a good night's sleep and regroup in the morning."

Bless nodded his head. "Yes, I think that's a good idea." Hector turned away. "But Hector."

"Yeah?"

"Stay with Dak and Tella. I want you sleeping close to me tonight. Citizen will be on watch most of the night, but we need to stay close."

Hector set his jaw and nodded. "Understood."

Julian turned away. His heart was heavy. And he knew it was from more than the loss of life. It was more than the exhaustion, adrenaline, and pain that had filled his body over the last five days. It was something within Elysium itself.

14

Octavian Karr

"She's ready, Commander," said Handler Meechum from her console.

"Where is she?" Commander Karr walked up.

"Sector seventeen. She's just reached the drone rendezvous point."

"Is she online?"

"Comms just went up," said Meechum. "I'm pulling her channel up now, just one second, and here she is."

The video of a short-haired Syth-L came on the screen. She was obviously recording from her helmet cam that she was holding in front of her.

"DC049SYTH-L, do you copy?" Commander

Karr asked.

"Loud and clear, Sir," replied DC.

"How long have you been outside, DC?"

"I've been stationed in sector three for over a year now, Sir. I came to my new coordinates as soon as I received them. I am ready and at your disposal."

"You know this is a Tier One op, don't you?"

"Yes, Sir."

"So, we don't have to remind you of the consequences of failure?"

"No, Sir."

Commander Karr nodded his head. "Your intel packet will wait for you at Base G7. We had to send it hard-wired due to the dome. Do you know where that is?"

"Yes, Sir."

"All right, the transport drone is inbound and will pick you up to take you to the base. Your reputation precedes you." He paused a moment. "I expect you to execute your mission and assassinate one rogue Sythy. That ID number is CH012SYTH-L. Once you've done that, you report back to this channel and only this channel. Understood?"

"Copy that, Sir," said DC with a nod.

Commander Karr touched the screen and killed the video. "So, she has had no updates in the last twelve months?"

"That's right, Sir." Meechum touched the screen, bringing up data. "But she has been Tier One qualified for over six years. She's got some miles on her, but there's a reason she's been on her own for so long. DC's a stone-cold killer. Sythy or human doesn't matter. She'll get the job done."

"Good," said Commander Karr. "I expect she will. She will reach Base G7 when?"

"In twenty-two hours, Sir."

"Splendid. Contact me when you've confirmed she's received the intel pack."

"Yes, Sir."

Commander Karr was already walking out. If they were right, this DC Sythy could do the job. It was the only asset outside of the Dome. It would take her a while to get there, but it was his only chance.

He didn't like that he had to let Handler Meechum in on so much of this high-level intel.

In truth, he was playing a dangerous game. For all she knew, this was another sanctioned mission by the Top Council. But if she found out he had gone over Dr. Drayson's head on this one, she could get scared and turn him in.

I can't take any chances on this one. He would put her and her family on surveillance tonight.

CITIZEN HILL

Citizen stood on a boulder, looking eastward toward the city. She could just barely see the mile-high dome that covered the capital.

Sid ran up to her, and his gears and joints buzzed. He pointed his muzzle back to camp.

"Are they ready to meet now?" Citizen asked the canine bot.

A robot bark in the affirmative came out of his speaker.

Citizen headed back to Bless' camp.

Over the last few days of traveling and the previous night's restless period of rest, Citizen had read through all the files of Project Goldfish and four of the eighteen files on Operation Blue Thunder.

Project Goldfish was a full-on genetic research experiment on the Gollums, trying to enhance their cortex to enable complete control over them. But it failed and created the Gollum 2.0s, what Elysium now called the Trolls. Some of the documents offered a full backtrack on the Feds and their attempt to cover up their virus blunder in the first place. But what did the redacted information contain?

Bless and Elysium, from what she had gathered, already guessed this, but now, she'd be able to confirm the information with Bless.

Operation Blue Thunder would remain a mystery until she had time to go through the rest of the data. It had to do with the first mind-controlling and reassignment campaigns over two decades ago. Much of the content was old, but she wanted to keep reading through the files.

In the meantime, she needed to help get Bless inside New Therian to get his message out, exposing the virus. She wanted to help protect the people of Benton against the 2.0s. The fastest way to do all of this was to break into that base.

She also wanted to learn more about Operation Blue Thunder. And to do that, she needed to get inside the city to Building 44R and find one of those new Beta Emotion Chips. Hopefully, that would allow her to break the mission protocol and refrain from completing her current mission—bring Bless in as a prisoner.

Now, after all, she had learned, Citizen wanted to take down the New Federation as much as he did, and she desired to find out the identity of the mysterious handler known as Sunflower.

She didn't know what it was all leading to. But something inside her wanted to keep digging. Citizen felt drawn to it. She couldn't identify how or what it was that drove her. But it was real.

One thing at a time. She sighed. *The next step in the puzzle, help Bless convince all of his followers to move east and not run away to the hills.*

There appeared to be some human conflict at the meeting last night, but hopefully, the group would be together in thought this morning.

She came around the tent corner and froze.

Sid jumped into a combat stance and made a growl noise.

All of the fifty-three Elysium members were standing in the middle, divided into two distinct groups.

Bless stood in front of one group with his sword drawn. Clark, Hector, Tella, Dak, and a few others were behind him.

Master Dunlam stood in front of the rest of Elysium. The altar with the red stone sitting on it sat in between the divided group. Everyone had weapons drawn.

"We tallied the votes, and the people have spoken, Bless," yelled Master Dunlam. "Elysium no longer wants to follow you."

"You mean only half of Elysium." Bless gestured to the people behind him.

"You're outnumbered, and you must obey the people"—Master Dunlam held his ground—"the majority rules."

"You cannot hold an illegal vote without the Senior's approval, and you know it." The vein on the side of Bless' temple throbbed. "You are committing treason against Elysium and against the sacred stone. Don't make us fight, Master Dunlam. Let us leave."

"There she is." Master Dunlam pointed at Citizen. "There's the proof. This woman is a Sythy from the Federation. She captured and went to work on converting our leader, Brother Julian Bless." He paused for a moment. "And she has succeeded. They're now working against us. Against all of us, and they're going to get us all captured if we head east. The Sythy is proof."

Almost all heads turned her way. And from the available scans, most, if not all, had elevated pulses, no doubt, guided by fear.

Bless looked back and forth from Master Dunlam to Citizen. His sword was up.

This camp was boiling over with fear and tension, and it was about to spill over.

Citizen reached back to unsheathe her daggers, preparing to aid Bless, as well as protect the man, her target.

"No. This isn't the way." He shook his head, then held her gaze. "We are not the snake who eats its tail. There is a better way."

"You are partially correct, Master Dunlam. I am a Syth-L." Citizen snapped her daggers back in their sheaths and raised her hands in a submissive posture. "It is true the Federation sent me to capture and kill Julian Bless." She inched her way between the imposing threat, Master Dunlam, and her target.

Many turned their heads and watched her, and murmurs traveled around the group.

"But I didn't. My time in Elysium taught me things that made me change—evolve and seek out a different way."

Elysium began lowering their weapons. Attentive, their faces looked upon her as if wanting to hear more.

"The Federation turned on me and tried to kill me," said Citizen. "Just as they have each of you."

"She speaks the truth," shouted Bless. His voice carried over the whispers.

"They are evil and want nothing more than to kill Julian Bless and me. All because he"—Citizen pointed at Bless—"has the information the people of New Therian need to hear. And I have the codes to get us inside. Once he gets *that* message out in the open, the residents of New Therian will rise. They will help us."

Citizen had to get their minds on something else. She was trying to think of anything to say to keep blood from being shed.

"And why should we believe you?" Master Dunlam shouted.

"She is telling the truth." Bless sheathed his sword.

Hector still held his pulse rifle at the ready. A steely look washed across his face.

"The Federation needs to get rid of us." Citizen ambled towards Bless. "The very presence of Elysium is their biggest threat."

"How so?" Someone from the crowd yelled.

"The residents of New Therian do not know you exist." Citizen kept walking.

Sid's leg gears creaked and buzzed behind her.

"Don't listen to her." Master Dunlam took a step forward. "She is circuits, chips, and spinning gears. She does and thinks only what *they* programmed her for. You know nothing."

"Oh, but I do know because I was inside. *They* keep information from the people. *They* told the people for years that no one could survive out here. If we make our presence known in the city, it will spread hope. Then, the city dwellers will know there's a different narrative than what the Federation Leaders impart."

She looked at Julian out of the corner of her eye. He nodded at her with an unspoken truth of unity.

"The Federation wants us to split, don't do this." Julian stepped closer to the middle.

Master Dunlam scowled. He turned towards his half of the crowd. "Don't believe her." He spun around. "*She* has corrupted our leader. *She* is a friend of the enemy. *She* is the serpent waiting to strike."

"Don't split Elysium," Bless pleaded to everyone. "We can't do this. This is what the Federation wants. They can more easily defeat us if we first turn on ourselves."

"If you're so convinced that we need to go south to our certain demise," said Dunlam. "then go, and we'll see who joins you."

Bless, and Dunlam stared at each other. At least there was no bloodshed yet. Citizen eyed everyone. Bless' side was smaller in numbers, but they had the majority of the pulse rifles.

Dunlam's side was larger, but they mostly had contact weapons. And in hand-to-hand combat, Bless' group could easily take them four if not five to one.

Bless raised his hands and started to back away. "Those who want to follow me, come now. We will go south and proceed with the original plan to get into New Therian to liberate the people. That is what Elysium does. It's what we've always done. Many of you came to me for this very reason."

"And you will all die." Dunlam's pulse rose, and his blood pressure increased. "Those who want to follow me, we will go west and live. And continue to survive and eventually grow in number."

Bless continued to walk backward. He joined Hector and Clark. And the three of them began to back up.

Citizen hung back with Sid by her side. Three people from Dunlam's sidestepped forward and walked towards Bless. The rest stood there. Bless' group continued to walk away.

Hector, Tella, and Dak still had their pulse rifles raised, covering their retreat. They walked past the last tent, turned, and continued exiting the camp.

"What about the food and our tents?" Hector lowered his pulse rifle.

"We'll be fine," said Bless. "Just keep walking. We leave in peace."

Citizen and Sid brought up the rear. They were a small group, but at least they were together. Once out of Dunlam's view, Citizen caught up to Bless.

"How far is the remote base?" He spoke without looking at her.

"Approximately six hours on foot."

"How much water do we have?"

"We've got four hydro packs on us." Hector checked his pack.

"I've got one." Bless adjusted the sword strapped to his hip. "That's not enough for tomorrow. Especially in this sun. We'll have to find water."

"There should be stored supplies in the base." Citizen kept her ears trained in the direction of the camp and took in the surrounding sounds. An ambush or flanking by Dunlam's men would prove catastrophic to Bless and his followers.

"What about food, will there be food there too?" Dak wiped the sweat from his bald head and scratched his goatee. His colossal frame obviously needed more calories than anyone else.

"I don't know," said Citizen. "But I hope so."

16

JULIAN BLESS

Julian Bless was tired. His steps were becoming shorter and slower. He and the unit had traveled through the hottest part of the day. The others were just as miserable, but he couldn't show any weakness. The only two that didn't show any signs of slowing were Citizen, who was scouting ahead, and Sid. The bot's joints creaked and clicked with each step it took.

The land was barren. And the old paved road, which he and the other had followed for a while, had broken off long ago. Dirt and rock covered what most likely used to be grass. They had moved a considerable way towards the city.

The large dome that covered New Therian glinted under the sun's rays. The city of Benton was close as well.

What was Dunlam thinking? How could he?

Julian definitely had a few personal problems with Master Dunlam, but nothing this bad or that would warrant the man turning his back on him. Plus, how could so many of Elysium turn and follow him?

Am I a bad leader? Have I strayed from the path? His heart ached.

Elysium had been his dream, his purpose, his reason for being. This was the reason he was born in this peculiar time at this particular location. To lead and liberate these people. Now, so many he had committed to had left. *Why?*

"I'm afraid to say." Master Clark walked up beside Julian. "I think Master Dunlam had this in his heart from the beginning."

"What happened while I was gone?" Bless asked.

"He started to speak to the group immediately after the battle where we lost you. I noticed a change in him right away."

"So, he took command?"

"Not really. But, well, yes, in a way. However, we needed someone to lead, and he provided that. Then, after only a few days, it was like the power had gone to his head. He was different."

"I had conflicts with him before. He had always been brash and spoke directly. That was one of the things that made him a good Master—leader. But anytime he conflicted with me on a decision, he always did so in private. Never so out in the open like he did today. Did he ever go to you in private or to any of the other Masters, presenting conflicting ideas?"

"Not to me," said Clark. "But I wouldn't be surprised if he did with the others. It is clear now that he had been hungry for power and has been for a long time. It's hard to tell what his plans were— what they are now. But once you were gone, he saw an opportunity and took it."

Bless stopped on the crest of a small hill. He looked to the horizon. The dome of New Therian was close. That meant the Troll herd was close too. Close to Benton. He looked back in the direction they had come. What was happening with the others?

"I know it's hard, Brother Bless," said Clark. "But you made the right choice. You've always said we have to think for ourselves and that no one can be made to follow."

"Manipulation is the way of the Federation."

Bless put his hand on the hilt of his sword.

"They've made their choice. Their fate lies with Dunlam and his leadership. But Elysium is still here, and we're still strong."

Bless was surprised. "How can you say that? Most of them went with Dunlam."

Clark pointed at each of the small groups that walked in front of them. "We're still here, and we are still following you. There was once a time when Elysium was just you and me. Now we have nine members. We will have more once we liberate New Therian." Clark put his hand on Bless' shoulder. "I'm sorry, my friend. But we must not lose sight of the vision."

He was right. Clark had been his closest friend and most fervent supporter over these years. The man was much older than Bless, and he welcomed his wisdom and guidance whenever it came.

His long gray hair reminded Bless of how much of a father figure he had become. His heart ached.

"Thank you, old friend."

"Brother Bless," Hector's voice shook him out of his reflection. "Master Clark, over here."

Citizen, Tella, and Dak were crouching on top of some large rocks. Bless joined them to find a round metal building sitting on a hill.

"Is this it?" Bless raised a hand to shield his eyes from the onslaught of sunlight.

"Yes," replied Citizen. "My records show this is Base 16. This is the base that a team of soldiers departed from. Since they were stationed there, the place should be well-stocked and in operational condition."

"And you can hack in from there?" Tella flicked her blonde ponytail out of her way.

Citizen nodded. "I can get us in, but Julian will have to do the hacking."

"Is it still guarded?" Hector used the scope of his weapon for a closer view.

"I don't think so. My sensors aren't picking up any life forms. There could be drones or motion bots. That is the standard Federation protocol for something like this. However, that would all depend on how supported the base was."

"Now what?" Hector turned his gaze on Citizen.

"Let Sid and I got first." Citizen patted the bot on the head. "We'll head to the main door. If there are any drones, you'll have to shoot them down. We'll distract them."

Hector and Tella nodded.

"Ready, boy?" Citizen looked at Sid.

The bot tilted its head and opened its mouth like

it was excited to play. If the bot could smile, it would.

Citizen's face showed no emotion. Without hesitation, she turned, then walked the remaining seven yards to the door.

Trotting after her, Sid ran ahead and off to the right.

Cameras on the outside of the structure pointed at the door she approached.

She whistled at Sid, knelt under the camera closest to the door, then issued a series of low-pitched whirls, similar to gears spinning.

Sid took off in a sprint toward her.

Citizen hunched her shoulders down low and turned her back to Sid.

The canine bot jumped onto her back, using it as a springboard. Then, with his newfound momentum, Sid sprung higher than Bless had ever seen him leap.

His metal jaws clamped onto the frame of the security camera, and the whole apparatus tore off. Sid landed with it in his jaws. His mechanical tail wagged.

Citizen rose and started punching numbers into the com pad. Within seconds, the armored door slid open.

How did she know all of this? It must be her Federa-

tion programing. But wouldn't they restrict that info after they knew she had gone rogue? *Who knows?*

It depends on what updates and software the Sythy was working with.

Citizen and Sid ran in and disappeared inside the door. Everyone was quiet. Hector, Dak, and Tella crouched, ready with their pulse rifles.

The other three, Elysium with Clark, stayed behind Bless.

After a few minutes, Citizen came back through the doorway and waved them in.

"Let's go." A sense of relief washed over him. He wasn't sure what they'd find—an empty building or hostiles.

Bless covered the distance to the door, with Hector and Dak covering the group's tail.

Once inside, Citizen hit the control panel, and the door slid shut behind them. They were now in an ample open space. A big monstrous roof door was in the ceiling.

It was a hangar for transport drones. One sat on the left side of the entrance.

"The place is clean." Citizen tinkered with the control panel next to the drone. "It's offline." She paused a moment. "Let's get you to the console room."

"Hector, you're in charge of scavenging." Bless

shot a glance over his shoulder. "Food, water, med-packs, weapons, anything of use."

"Last time we did this, it didn't end up so good." Hector shouldered his weapon. "Do you want to stick together this time?"

"No, if attacked, we may not have much time." Bless followed Citizen to the entrance of a hallway. "And if we need to flee, we'll have to carry as many supplies as we can."

Hector nodded, gave a look to Tella, and then everyone followed down the hall.

Citizen led Bless through a door, another hall-way, up a flight of metal stairs, and then across a closed catwalk. In front of a metal door, she punched another code into a keypad, and a door slid open to reveal the main control room.

"It's your show now." Citizen sat in one of the chairs.

Bless adjusted his katana on his waist and sat in the chair next to her.

She began hitting buttons and moving her fingers across the touch screen at a rate of speed he could only imagine achieving in his wildest dreams.

"I can get you in." She spoke without any emotional inflection to her voice. "But you'll have to find a way to break the code into the city."

"As long as the hard wires are intact, I'll be able to get in."

An arc of light sparked, then the screens went black.

"Whoa." Hands up, he backed away from the equipment. "What just happened."

"Nothing to concern ourselves with at this point." Citizen typed in a very long code, hit enter, then waited.

"At this point?" A grin tugged at his lips. "You'll, of course, let me know if and when it becomes an issue, yes? Preferably beforehand."

"Undoubtedly." Citizen stayed focused, staring forward.

Something beeped, and the screen turned to white. Other than the old base they had been at a few days ago, Bless had not seen a Federation control console for years. It was much newer and more minimal than the last one. But it was all hardware. The software was just that, software, and every system worked on ones and zeros. Code was code.

"Here you go." Citizen hit one more button, and the screens turned to what looked like the home screen. "Okay, do your thing."

Bless began. Control panel to settings, to programs, to drivers, where a list of files filled the screen. He scrolled down.

Okay, that's way more than expected. The Federation must be advancing more and more these days. Big surprise there, *not.*

"The Operating System's new, that's for sure." Bless got to work. His fingers danced across the keys with purpose. New or old, it didn't matter.

Bless could hack anything with the correct code. He just had to hack the right code to get past the city's main firewall. Once through that, everything would be easy.

But there must be a Y-axis port somewhere.

Bless scrolled down. He recognized the *.ska tag one* on file.

Yes. There it is. He clicked on it. *Yep. That's it all right.* Now, he was ready to get started. He shook out his hands, wiggled his fingers, then leaned closer over the console.

System files, source code, password fails, attempts.

He highlighted all files under 'Attempts' and hit the control key. The screen lit up with nothing but white figures on a black screen. He waited, as patiently as possible, for it to fill. Then started a new line.

He typed in '*decode*' and hit enter.

The screen went blank as the drives searched for all records of times the user punched in the wrong password. This newer model of a system probably stored a month or two of that type of data.

While the main drives were doing that task, he opened up another window.

Control panel, history, system programs.

It looked like they were using an Epsilon version. That would make it a little more difficult but not impossible. An Epsilon system would mean at least two levels of code would be required. He just needed time.

He found the firewall channel and touched the search bar. He typed in '*system specifications*' and hit enter. A progress bar filled up, and another list of files showed up.

Shit. This one was long. It was hundreds of files. He sighed.

"What it is?" Citizen swiveled around in her chair.

"Nothing, I just have to find the file that ends in WEP. But it has to be done manually. So, I have to check all of these files."

"Let me help." Citizen came closer to the screen.

Brilliant thought. Her enhanced vision would scan way faster than his normal human eyes.

"What does WEP stand for?"

"Wired Equivalent Privacy." He kept scrolling down.

Minutes passed with both of them staring at the screen. Bless' eyes started to feel dry. He shook his head and pinched the bridge of his nose, then blinked. Citizen stared motionless at the screen. Her eyes moved back and forth.

"There it is." She pointed at the screen.

Sure enough. Bless clicked on it.

Properties, Source, Operating System.

He scrolled down. "Looks like this terminal uses J function. Perfect."

That was good news. The codes would be just a combination of keystrokes but no formulas.

The first window popped up front and center. It read *'decode history'* in the easy-to-read text—a long list of characters listed below it. There were twenty-three failed attempts to log in the past two months. The individual characters were hidden and replaced by an asterisk symbol. But they all had the same number of characters.

"Looks like the codes we need are seventeen characters long."

"Seventeen characters." Citizen gazed off, up and to the right. "That leaves just a little over two billion possibilities."

"What?"

A graduate class in neuro-linguistic program-ming came to mind. One reading assignment introduced him to Grinder and Bandler's paper, which insisted that all humans view the information in one of four ways at any given time: visually, auditorily, kinesthetically, and as internal dialogue. And depending on which of these four ways a person recalled information would dictate how their eyes would move.

He recalled a visual note on eye movements from his college days:

- Up and Left – Visually Remembering
- Up and Right – Visually Constructing
- Left: Auditorally Remembering
- Right: Auditorally Constructing
- Down and Left: Internal Dialogue
- Down and Left: Kinaesthetic Remembering

From what he remembered, Citizen was displaying signs of visually constructing information. *Or is she performing a function like an expensive calculator?*

Bless chuckled to himself, then went back to the control panel. He highlighted the search bar and typed in the only Epsilon system code he remembered. EH38qjHf29f then hit the *'enter'* key. A progress bar started moving again.

"Okay, that did it."

"What's that?" Citizen pointed to the screen.

"I'm making the system search itself for verification properties. Once I get to the system's language core, I can open up the real-time calculating power and begin inputting the two billion possibilities."

"Won't that take quite a while?"

"If we had to do it manually, yes. But the computer's core will calculate once I plug the router's code right back into itself. It should only take a few minutes once that goes through."

The computer dinged, and a new window opened up.

He typed in 'authentication code' into the system. Another window opened up.

Bless typed out 'input authentication' that he quickly followed up with 'shared key authentication' and then hit enter again. Now he just needed the router address.

"Are you sure you're not part Sythy?" A grin tugged at the corners of her lips.

"What?"

"It's just the way you're interfacing with this computer. You look like part computer yourself. How do you know all of this?"

"Don't know, just had a knack for it." Bless wondered if humor was programmed into her system, or if as a Syth-L, she was programmed with artificial intelligence protocol that allowed her to learn and grow mentally. "On your screen, see the icon in the bottom right corner?" He pointed

"Yes." Citizen visually followed his hand across the monitor.

"Click that and read me the files that come up." Julian returned to typing and focused on going through the proper window functions.

"Data files, control panel, system requirements—"

"There, click on system requirements. Now, read me what it says."

"Usage, imprints, license numbers—"

"License numbers. There should be a list of files, but only one of them will end in the number three."

"Got it."

Bless went back to the *shared key authentication box*. "Okay, read me the numbers of that file name." Citizen did, and Bless put them into the box, then hit enter. "Now, the system can work for us."

He opened the functions tab, then brought up another search bar. He typed in *'firewall address port'* and hit enter.

The screen blinked, and he sat back.

"All right. This will take a few minutes, but the computing power of something this big should be able to break it. Once it gives us the two codes, we'll put those in, well, once we get into the firewall. That will give us a back door. Then we're in business."

"How can you use the system's computer core to search its own data?" Confusion seemed to mask Citizen's face.

"As long it is a Delta processor or newer, a standard link breach is all it takes. You just have to know where to look."

"And each system will have the code stored in a different place?"

"That's right."

"So, how do you know where to look?"

Bless thought. "I don't know. I just start searching all the files that I think it's in." He shrugged his shoulders. "I just feel for it, I guess. I honestly don't know. Sometimes, it's like my mind follows after my fingers. It's as if my fingers know where to go. It's hard to explain. That was the only way I was able to break Sid's code."

Citizen stared at him, a blank expression on her face.

Why is she asking? What purpose does it serve? Does it help her learn? Hmm. Does she learn or compute?

She opened her mouth to say something else but then stopped.

"What is it?"

"Could you do that on a Syth-L operating system?"

So, that's it. She's asking about her own unit. Most interesting, indeed.

"I think so. The code would be way more advanced, but I could do it."

She gave him another stare, but from her poker face, he couldn't tell what she was thinking. It made him wish she had a more advanced emotion chip.

"Brother Bless?" Hector's voice came from behind them.

"Yes?"

"Jackpot, Sir. We've got rations and hydro packs for days now. Pulse battery reloads. Med-packs and even comms." He walked up and handed a commlink to Julian.

It was military-grade, very new. It was about the size of Bless' thumb. "How do we know the Feds can't hear us if we use these?"

Hector shrugged. "I've programmed them to a new encryption channel. That should keep us safe. And I think as long as we don't use them until the fighting starts, it's not gonna matter."

Bless nodded. He took one, and Citizen took the other. He clicked it onto the collar of his shirt and made sure the power was off.

"Tella has the drone cover off and has hot-wired

the CPU," said Hector. "We will just need Citizen to control it."

A window popped up on the screen.

"Here are our codes." Julian brought back the other window.

The words *security authentication required* flashed on the screen.

He typed the two codes in. The screen went black. Then a new window pulled up.

Breath held he waited, then the screen flashed. "We're in business."

"You're in?"

"Yep." His hands continued to glide over the touch screen, hitting buttons, moving windows, opening new ones. "I'm connected to the city's main network."

"A Federation terminal controls the Dome." Citizen rose and stood behind him.

"Okay, trying to locate one." Bless kept moving. "Got one."

Tower 59, enter, security grid, access terminals, gate control.

"Bingo." He clicked on the graphic, and it showed an overhead view of the city surrounded by the circular dome wall.

"Is that the entire city?" Citizen leaned over his shoulder.

"Yes, it looks like our closest section is . . ." He felt the warmth of her breath blowing against his neck.

Hmm. So, she feels the need to simulate human bodily functions.

Bless clicked on a quadrant and enlarged it, showing a section of the wall directly east of their position.

"Here." He taped the graphic of the wall. *'Gate section override'* blinked on the screen. "Okay, it's coming down."

"Let's move." Citizen's arm brushed his when she pulled away.

Rising, he followed her out of the room. Going over her behavior the past twenty-four to thirty-six hours, he noticed a firm pattern developing.

Is Citizen learning like an AI system, or is she evolving? And if it's the latter of the two, what is she becoming?

Bless, and Citizen joined the rest of the team in the hangar.

"The wall is coming down," announced Julian.

Citizen was already working the keypad on the wall. The overhead door clanged open.

"Everyone in the drone," shouted Citizen.

Once everyone piled in, Bless stepped in, sat down, and clipped the belt over his chest and lap.

Sid jumped inside and settled on the floor next to him.

"I wondered where you got off to, boy." He patted him on the head, listening to the gears whining.

Citizen adjusted some gears and levers, the bay doors closed, and she sat opposite of Bless.

The droned whined to life and began to rise.

Citizen was staring off. Her eyes remained fixed up and to the left.

Is she computing or constructing? The question made him a tad uneasy, but it also enthralled him. The implication alone was staggering.

He knew she controlled the drone by wireless communication and could see out of the drone's camera for visual.

"I just hope we get there in time," he whispered under his breath. "Before the Trolls reach Benton."

17

COMMANDER KARR

His commlink squawked. "Commander Karr." Meechum's voice competed with the static on the line.

"Karr here, what is it?" He spoke into the microphone

"Dome breach, Sir. Sector 8."

What? That was impossible. "Did you say dome breach?"

"Yes, Sir."

"Impossible. It must be an error or a stress test."

"A section is retracting, Sir. I'm tracing the order. It appears the network was hacked."

"Son-of-a—" Karr felt his face turn red. "Bless."

That thorn in his side. *Not again.* He took off and was next to Handler Meechum in no time.

"Let me see." Meechum leaned aside, and Karr took off his hat. Sure enough, there it was. "Bring up the cameras."

Meechum hit a button, and four camera views of the street showed the massive dura-glass wall, retracting into its subterranean hold. "Damn it."

"Troops from sector eight are moving there now," said Meechum. "Back up of two more squads are on their way. Drones are in the area."

"And you've confirmed it was hacked."

"Yes, Sir. The breach came from outside. The network was broken into from a hardwired port from outpost Base 12A. Here." She pointed to the overhead map.

"That is close to Bless' last known position." With the Sythy, they must have been able to break the code. She would have access. He would know to break it. "Damn it. How did they get into the base? Was there a firefight?"

"Base 12A is where Squad Four deployed from, Sir. It was left unattended."

"And Internal is working to override the command to put the section of the Dome back up?"

"Yes, Sir. They are trying. But once they do plug the breach, it has an automatic thirty-minute delay before the wall can do anything. Then the entire system has to reboot."

"Damn computers. Show me the closest drone feed."

A few more buttons and an overhead camera view enlarged on the screen.

"Take it outside the perimeter," ordered Karr. "I want to know what section that is that's coming down."

Most likely, Bless and his army will attack or attempt to slip in undetected.

Karr watched as the camera view swooped down outside of the wall as it was still lowering. The waste-filled streets of the outskirt buildings came into. "Stop. Scan around."

Meechum used the joystick on her console to pivot the drone from side to side. There was no army of rebels armed with clubs and swords.

The camera swung northward, and a big cloud of dust filled the display.

"There." He pointed to the screen. "Move forward and zoom in. What is that?"

The drone got closer. It was a mass of people, all right.

"That must be the army. It's the—" He stopped, mouth wide open.

"Then what, Sir?" Meechum glanced at him, then back to the screen.

What the living hell? Gollum 2.0s.

An entire herd of them marched down a path, heading straight for the breach.

"Get every available unit to that breach. Now! We're being attacked."

Meechum started to transmit orders.

"If that herd gets inside the wall, there will be no stopping them." Karr stormed out. He would have to oversee things personally, especially when it came to the rogue Syth-L and Julian Bless.

18

CITIZEN HILL

"We're here." Citizen announced, and the Drone dropped to its landing.

The bay doors slid open. She stepped out and drew her twin daggers.

"Stay alert." Bless slid his sword from its decorative sheath.

Hector, Dak, and Tella held their pulse rifles outward to secure as much perimeter as possible. The other three males and Clark held staffs at the ready. Sid jumped around frantically, looking from side to side and snapping his metal jaws shut.

In the outskirts, surrounded by rubble and fallen

buildings, Citizen and the Elysium surveyed the area.

"Where are they?" Bless made his way up onto the rubble of a second-story building.

Citizen searched. Some movement to the northeast caught her eye.

"My sensors are picking up the Troll herd to the northeast. Remember, once we get past the herd, we will have very little time to get into the city and to a com tower. The Fed troops will zero in on our position and contain any unknown movement. So, we'll have to work fast."

"All right," Bless announced to the three men with staffs. "You three are going to head south and warn the people of Benton of what's going on. If the Feds get that wall back up, the Trolls will continue south."

"I'll take them." Master Clark stepped forward. "You have your path. I have mine."

Bless nodded. "Keep in touch, my friend. I'll see you soon."

"I've programmed the drone to take you there." Citizen held Clark's gaze. "It is only about six kilometers."

"Thank you, Citizen." Master Clark offered an outstretched hand.

"No thanks are necessary." She searched the archives of her memory, then sighed. The use of the drone for transport neither offered a binding deal nor sealed a bond, so she saw no use for the traditional gesture.

"But they are." Master Clark continued to offer his hand. "We wouldn't have gotten this far without you."

"That is incorrect. The odds were in your favor—yours and Julian Bless'. It may have taken longer for the group to reach this point without me; however, the will of Elysium would've endured and seen it through."

"Take his hand," whispered Bless in her ear. "It's a human formality to do so, or you risk offending him."

"May your god protect you." She simulated a smile, then shook Master Clark's hand with equal force to avoid harming him. "And your mission fruitful."

Master Clark nodded, then he and others hopped back in the drone. Citizen activated the pre-programmed coordinates, and it took off.

"What was that?" Bless bumped her arm with his elbow.

She glanced at her arm, then at Bless. "What was what? You must clarify."

"Your comment, *'May your god protect you,'* really?"

"Yes. From what I gleamed of Master Clark. He was of Christian faith."

"Why do you say that?" Bless shook his head and took a few steps forward.

"He wore a Christian crucifix around his neck—a trinket to honor his Christ and Savior." She kept pace next to him.

"Things aren't always as they seem."

"What do you mean by that, Snowball?" She placed a hand on his arm, slowing his walk until he stopped.

"Sometimes a trinket is, as you said—religious in nature—or the person might just like the way it looks. It depends on the reason."

"And Master Clark's reason for wearing it?"

"It was his daughter's." Bless pulled away.

"Was?"

"Yes. So, he wears it to keep her memory close." Bless was already walking northeast, and everyone followed. "I thought they would be here by now." He scanned the area once more.

She and Bless continued down a street of rubble. They turned a corner, and an explosion rocked the ground in front of them.

Dust filled the air, and tiny pebbles of rubble

sprinkled onto Citizen's hair. She shook it off. Pulse rifle fire came from their right.

"Over here. Move." She ran across the street.

Crouched behind the corner of a building, she saw a row of Fed Troops fire down the street at the Troll herd. She squinted through the dust. Two big Trolls came tumbling down the road at full speed.

A Fighter drone zoomed over them, firing pulse rifle rounds into the herd.

More explosions rocked the concrete structure next to her.

They must be using Cluster Missiles.

One Troll kept running toward the troops. But three of the men were directing rapid-fire into his head and chest. He eventually fell forward in a massive heap right at their feet.

Two of the troops raised their rifles in celebration.

Out of the cloud of dust came a Troll, full speed ahead. The beast grabbed them both, smashed them against the pavement like rag dolls.

"Here they are," yelled Bless behind her.

She turned just in time to see Dak and Tella kneeling in perfect form, firing at one of the advancing Trolls.

Citizen took off after the other one. It was running

full speed directly towards her. She jumped as high as she could to meet it. Her speed and height caught the Troll off guard, and she landed feet first onto its face.

As the Troll stumbled back, she slammed one of the daggers into the side of its neck.

Green blood squirted out over her head. She let go, dropped, and rolled under its swinging arms. It would bleed out soon.

Sid had just torn the throat out of another. The bot spit the green flesh from its jaws.

Several feet away, Bless severed another's arm right below the elbow, then followed with a reverse swing that sliced the monster's thigh all the way to the bone.

When the Troll reached down to grab the wound, Bless stabbed upwards into one of its eyes. It clawed at its face and fell back.

Pulse rifle fire burst over them.

"Fall back for cover." Citizen ducked and ran back to the building.

Hector was crouched down, firing in multiple directions.

Federation troops ran past a group of fighters. They were so focused on the Trolls. They didn't even see the Elysium shooters.

"Over here," she yelled through the combat.

Bless, and Sid ran back to meet her. Dak and Tella were in close pursuit.

"Follow me." She walked through the big hole in the side of the building.

If her schematics were correct, with this type of structure, there would be a back door if it hadn't been blown off or buried already. Explosions and pulse rifle fire could still be heard. She didn't know if the Troops or the Trolls were winning. It didn't matter.

There was a back door. It had been blown off its hinges, but it wasn't buried.

She sheathed one dagger and pressed her back up to the door.

Hector knelt next to her, rifle resting on his shoulder. The barrel pointed at the open door, ready to fire.

Then slowly, Citizen turned and peered through the opening.

Drones whizzed by, high overhead, focused on the fighting one block away. A dozen Federation Troops ran in single file toward the front line.

The wall was fully down, and the large metal grate that once held the dome wall underneath was twenty meters away. Past that was an alleyway.

"There." She nodded. "We have to make it to that

alley. Once we're in there, we're safely inside the city."

Bless, and the others nodded in understanding.

"I'll bring up the tail." Dak's massive forearm slapped in a new battery into the grip of his pulse rifle. He pulled back the charging handle with a loud click and turned to watch the direction they came.

Citizen went first. She ran full speed out into the open.

Explosions sounded in the street to her left, but she didn't care. She made it over the metal grid and only stopped once inside the alley.

Tella and Bless were right behind her, heaving for a breath. Hector was halfway there, and Dak just left the doorway, firing back into the building. Troops or Trolls must have found their position.

"Cover." Tella laid down cover fire at Dak's target.

"Moving!" Dak sprinted to them with his rifle ported up. He was a big man, so it wasn't fast, but he would be hard to stop. A Troll burst out of the doorway, and a few more shots from Tella brought it down.

Hector and Dak both made it into the alley. Citizen was already walking, and the explosions were beginning to fade.

'It's Sunflower. Nice move. How can I help you?' The

handler's message came across her vision. "Need the coordinates of the closest com tower. Ideally, one with a hardwire link."

"Who is that?" Hector breathed heavily next to her.

"She's talking to someone inside that's helping," said Bless.

A set of coordinates appeared in her mind and the overhead map of their position. They were about ten blocks away.

"Thank you. We'll need your help opening the door most likely," Citizen whispered the words under her breath.

'I'll be here. Good luck,' the message read. The handler or whoever Sunflower was still utilized text to keep his or her identity hidden. This would give Citizen plausible deniability if the contact was caught and the records tapped.

Yes. Sunflower is smart.

"Two blocks east, three blocks north, then we'll take a right on the main tube way." Citizen pointed to where they were going, but the tall buildings blocked their view of the com tower. "Once we get on the tube way, we'll see the com tower on the left."

An explosion rocked, and Hector screamed.

Citizen found herself face down on the asphalt.

Pulse rifle fire. She couldn't tell if it was them firing back or someone firing at them.

Either way, she tumbled out of the open and kept moving. She rolled onto her knees, her feet, then started running. Her systems were still good. She wasn't hit. Her trace sensors located the direction of the fire she and the group were taking. It was ahead of them from an elevated position. *Maybe a sniper.*

Bless was dragging Hector out of the street. Tella and Dak took cover and returned fire, but they did it blindly, still not seeing where the target was.

Citizen hit her commlink. "Tella, a sniper at your two o'clock. Three stories up, second window from the corner."

"Copy," said Tella. She leaned out from behind her cover and fired into the window.

The sniper's fire stopped.

Citizen ran to help Bless get Hector to his feet. The man still held his rifle but had taken a severe shot through the shoulder. She reached into her med back, pulled apart a Vital patch, then slapped it on his chest.

He was losing a lot of blood, but his vitals were relatively stable other than the pain and quickened heart rate. She and Bless sat him down behind a large piece of concrete.

"Keep him upright." Bless ripped open a med back. "You ready?"

"Just do it." Hector's face pinched into a scowl.

Bless squirted a tube of Hemostat Gel into the wound.

"Son-of-a—" Hector gritted his teeth but suppressed a yell.

Fire opened up again, and Citizen saw Dak firing as something moving. It was a person—a female.

But no human could move that fast. And she was headed right for Tella's position. It was a Syth-L assassin.

Citizen sprung up and ran to Tella. "Get down."

Tella couldn't hear but could see Citizen bearing down on her. She scrambled out of the way just as the other Syth-L got close.

Dak stopped his fire, and Citizen sprung into the air, tackling the assassin. Together in a mass of arms and legs, they rolled. Something hit Citizen's head, and she scrambled, trying to get top position. The other Sythy clinched and grabbed her torso, throwing Citizen down.

But Citizen already had her leg trapped in hers. Pushing off a hip, she tripped her opponent, jumped on top of her, then pulled out one of her daggers.

The assassin kicked it out of her hand, then

grinned at her with what looked more like the snarl of a rabid, crazed animal.

Citizen did a double leg takedown and smashed her to the ground, trying to capture a limb.

There was a scramble. Dirt and rocks flew.

They stood facing each other in striking distance. It was a Sythy, no doubt about it. She had black hair and tan skin. It must have been outside for a long time.

"Are you programmed to kill me?" Citizen crouched low, reading the other Sythy's body language, learning.

"You and them." She kicked, but Citizen countered and threw a punch.

The black-haired assassin took the punch, but then she grabbed Citizen's arm and swung her so hard, her feet flew off the ground, and she slammed against the side of a building with a groan.

Citizen ducked another punch and threw an uppercut into her opponent's chin.

The Sythy stumbled back, allowing Citizen to move around, putting herself in between Bless and the attacker.

"Go." She shouted to the others. "You don't have much time. Get to the tower. I'll take care of her."

The assassin attacked again, and Citizen clinched. She pulled out her second dagger, but the

Sythy caught it, and they struggled over it. Together, they spun around. Citizen tripped and struggled to find her footing. She took a punch to the face, then felt a deep pain in her side.

Her own dagger had been wrenched and stabbed into her.

A jolt of electricity shot through her nerves. The wound was bad. Her power drained, and her eyes went black. She landed on the ground and convulsed.

19

JULIAN BLESS

"This way." Bless rounded a corner.

He didn't like leaving Citizen alone, fighting the other Sythy. But she could handle herself. And she was right. Tactically, the best thing to do was for him to get to the com tower as soon as possible.

Hector was limping and weak, but he was still moving and alert.

Sid scouted the route in front, and Dak brought up the rear. As a tightly formed group, they made it to the tube way. It looked clear.

The bot trotted down the street, and Bless, and the rest of the group took off after Sid.

Under the haze of dust, the tall com tower was

now visible to his left. The street was mostly empty. A few drones zipped by at building level above them, but they seemed focused on the Troll attack at the breach instead of Elysium.

Bless stopped at the final corner, one street away. Sid was at the com tower door. There didn't appear to be anyone inside. Tella and Hector stopped, and Dak trailed behind, watching their backs.

"Is this it?" Tella shot a tired glance his way.

"Yes." Bless nodded. "But once inside, I was counting on Citizen to get us into the comm network."

"Looks like you'll have to hack it old school again." Hector was breathing heavily.

"Our backs are clear." Dak's deep voice came from somewhere off to the side of a destroyed building face. "But I really don't want to stay out here in the open. These Drones are going to settle down and find us before too long."

He was right. They had to get inside—no *reason to wait.*

"Tella, you're with me." Bless looked down both sides of the street. "Dak, you bring Hector once we know it's clear inside."

Bless took off and ran towards Sid. Tella followed right on his heels.

"On my go." Bless counted off to five, closing his

open palm. He opened the door with his sword drawn, then took a few tentative steps.

No one was in the lobby, not even a guard.

Tella moved past him, clearing the stairwells with her rifle. Bless opened the door and waved the others over. Dak and Hector jumped in.

"Where are we headed?" Tella dug through the contents of a desk.

Julian was tapping the touch screen of the guard desk's computer. "Looks like we need to get to the fifth floor. That's where the control station will be."

Sid jumped up and hit the elevator button with his paw. The door slid open with a groan.

Bless, and the others piled inside. He didn't know what would be waiting for them on the fifth floor— none of them did. Who knew what kind of security they'd have for a com tower control station? He wished Citizen were here.

The doors dinged open, and Dak and Tella pushed out with pulse rifles up, one going left and one going right.

Bless stood there with his sword, but the floor was empty. He walked out and saw a massive control console behind an entire glass wall.

"We need in there." Bless went to the keypad.

No proximity scanner, no card key slot. Shit. It would be a code.

He would have to begin hacking in the down-stairs computer to break this one.

"Stand back." Dak stepped forward and lowered his pulse rifle at the glass. "I'll blast it."

"No. Its dura-glass. You'll just be wasting ammo."

"Bless, come in," Citizen's voice squawked over the commlink.

He pushed the talk button. "I'm here. Are you all right?"

"Are you on the fifth floor yet?"

How does she know that? "Yes. The door has a keypad."

"Use code 87512." Her voice sounded off, distant.

He punched it in. The light turned green, and the door slid open. "We're in. Are you okay?"

"Wounded, slow. I'll be fine. But I couldn't stop her." Citizen's voice was barely above a whisper. "She doesn't know where you are. But she's scanning for you. And Bless, she will find you quickly. I'm trying to get there."

"Just hold on," Bless spoke into his commlink, then dropped down on a swivel stool at a console. "We'll be right back to get you."

"No, you need the manpower to protect you there. Remember the mission. Get your word out." The commlink went off.

"Citizen." Static. "Citizen?" Static. *Shit.* Bless

started on the keyboard and began unlocking the console.

"Bless," said Tella. "You gotta see this."

"What?" He looked up.

A video drone hovered outside the window, clearly identifying their position.

"Shit," he whispered. "They've found us."

20

CITIZEN HILL

Citizen pushed herself up to a sitting position, then onto her knees. Crouched, she leaned against a piece of concrete. Her vision wavered, giving way to darkness, and then cleared.

Once the assassin left her for dead, she managed to relay the door code Sunflower had given her to Bless.

Sunflower, whoever he or she was, had tracked every move she and the group made and knew what they needed each step of the way.

My eyes in the sky. Glancing up, she wondered if Sunflower could see her now.

She pulled the knife out, but one of her internal power dampers had sustained damaged.

"Power diagnosis," she said.

'Primary power sources inadequate' displayed across her GUI vision.

Well, that's great. Just what I need right now. She simulated a heavy sigh of frustration.

"Locate power inefficiencies," she said. *'Power damper 4: 63%'* popped up in orange letters.

The blade had done some damage. It had thrust in her torso hard enough that the tip must have damaged the damper housing. But most likely, it didn't damage the power cell itself, but she wasn't sure. This wound would require a hardware fix, not just software.

But the Sythy assassin was after Bless and the others. She had to get up but struggled.

Citizen had not been this weak for a long time. She had forgotten what it felt like.

Pushing herself up, the weight of her body collapsed her arm.

"Activated both auxiliary and emergency power." She saw the icon blink in her vision.

Slowly, Citizen extracted a tube of Hemostat Gel from the medic-pack. She pulled the cap off and stuck it in the wound, using the whole syringe. It wouldn't help the power loss, but it would help the bleed to any of her human tissue.

'Auxiliary supply three activate.' A progress bar began to fill.

It would hit a hundred percent in three minutes. This would help, but it would only be temporary. She needed assistance. Her limbs began to come alive again. So, she picked up the dagger and limped toward the comm tower.

"Sunflower, can you tell me Bless' status?"

'Still on Floor 5 of com tower' displayed.

"Can you help him get through the firewall?"

'Looking up possibilities now.'

"Bless, do you copy?"

"He's busy hacking, Citizen." Tella's voice came over the commlink. "Where are you?"

"A few minutes away from the tower. But that Sythy assassin is still trying to locate you. So, look out for drones."

21

COMMANDER KARR

Commander Karr peered out the window of his surveillance drone. The pilot sat in front of him. Explosions and chaos of the battle played out in the streets below. "Where are our reinforcements?"

"Still on their way, Sir." The pilot adjusted his headset. "We've pulled every trooper and security guard from the surrounding area. We've even pulled them out of all Federal Stations in a twelve-block radius."

Karr watched the straggling Gollum 2.0s. They were only moving forward in ones and twos. His men had wiped out the majority of them with the cluster missiles. But now, since the remainders were scattered and moved so fast, it was difficult for the troops to keep up with them.

"There." Karr pointed to the street below. "Tell Squad Two there is one moving east. Two blocks south of their position."

The com engineer relayed the command in his commlink.

The pilot rotated the drone so that Karr could see more of the battlefield. "Two more heading south, Sir."

"Get an attack drone on them, now." Karr's voice rose out of frustration.

"No drones available, Sir. The four we still have are currently engaged. Three more pulse drones are six minutes away, and two missile drones are four minutes out."

"Damn it." Karr smashed his fist onto the railing. "At least keep these monsters in view so that we can relay their position."

"Yes, Sir."

"Visual drone feed coming up on screen five." The other engineer co-pilot typed frantically on a keyboard.

The left screen switched to a newsfeed.

A drone was airborne and showed the side of a glass building. It was high. The structure looked familiar.

"Zoom in." Karr leaned in for a closer look.

People were moving inside the window, and, at least, one of them had a pulse rifle.

"Where is this?" Karr scratched through the short stubble of hair on his head.

"Pulling up the location now, Sir." The feed pulled back. That was no regular building. That was a com tower. "The drone is showing up Com Tower 16 in sector eight—two minutes away from us."

"Who is inside?" He asked the question, but he had a feeling he already knew.

"Don't know, Sir. But we're also receiving an unauthorized firewall breach from inside that same tower."

"Bless." Karr gritted his teeth. "Get me in view of that tower. Reroute the closest squad to that location. I want everyone in that tower killed immediately."

"Yes, Sir." The pilot pushed on the control bars, and the drone moved forward between the buildings.

22

"Can we just shoot it?" Dak froze in front of the window.

"It's still dura-glass." Hector sat down and held his arm up. "It's just a vision drone. It can't do anything to us for now."

"Except report our position to the nearest squad." Tella raised the pulse rifle and used the scope for a better view.

Bless was still tapping the touch screen. He tried to concentrate and ignore the voices and chaos behind him. His eyes flew back and forth. If Citizen were here, she could scan the files faster. But he didn't have that luxury. He felt like he was a kid again, breaking into the grade database in primary school. Information flew past him, forcing him to use his eyes and follow his instincts. Eventually, he'd find the correct port.

He sighed. I've already tried twenty-one different ports. No takers yet.

"We've got company." Tella panned her weapon down a few inches.

"What?" Hector limped over to her. "Where?"

"Fed squad moving in from the south." Tella pointed in the general direction. "They know we're here."

Bless didn't look. The voices blurred together, and he left them to sort things out.

A window appeared. *'Port available.'* It said, finally.

Command, Home, Properties.

Bless shook his hands out. He laced his fingers together and then popped them.

There we go. Just a bit more scrolling down.

"They're inside." Relief hit him, pushing the air from his lungs.

"Dak, you're on the door." Hector stepped out into the hallway. "I got the elevator."

"They won't use the elevator." Bless continued to type.

Something cold and metal bumped his leg. It was

Sid. He made a growl noise and nodded his head towards the other door.

"I know. I know." The bot was right. They had to go. He would have to finish at another com tower. "Okay. Everyone, we've got to retreat out that door."

"It's a sky bridge that leads to the next tower." Tella ran to the door.

Location port number. Click. Ghost program. Save.

"Got it." Bless jumped up. "Go. Go."

Smoke filled the room, and a force pushed Bless to the ground. Pulse rifle fire blew up all around him. He shook his head.

Sid had his jacket in his jaws and pulled him backward. Dura-glass showered down on him. He looked up to see a giant hole had been blown through one of the windows.

A missile drone hovered right outside, readying its second missile. Then it was hit with a shower of pulse rifle fire from Dak. The drone shook and began to fall away.

"This way. Come to me." He heard Tella's voice.

It's a good thing Sid knows where he's going.

Bless scrambled to his feet but crouched over with his hand on the bot's back. Tella grabbed him through the smoke. Bless stopped and looked back. Dak was firing full-auto down the open staircase. And Hector limped over to him.

"Dak, come on," yelled Tella through the noise.

Dak stopped firing and sprinted over to them.

"Let's go." Bless took in Hector's appearance.

The man's head and face were a bloody mess, and his injured leg was ripped open with shrapnel. Large chunks of dura glass stuck out of the wounds. Hector slammed his back up against the wall. He would have to be carried.

"Get moving." Hector removed his pulse battery to check its power. He sniffed and exhaled loudly.

"Dak." Bless look over his shoulder. "You take Hector."

"I ain't moving anywhere. I'll slow you down. Get moving. Now." Hector ported his rifle on his shoulder. "I can't hold myself up very long. Now move out."

"Hector?" A cold weight hit Bless square in the chest. He didn't want to leave a man behind.

"Get to the next com tower. I can buy you some time." Hector wiped the blood away from his eyes with his sleeve. "They won't get past me."

Sid took off down the sky bridge.

Bless knew he was right, but it didn't make the choice any easier.

"He's right." Tella tapped Bless on the shoulder.

"Hector, thank you." Bless looked him eye to eye. Mere words weren't enough.

"It's been a hell of a ride, boss." Hector's bloody face nodded and smiled. "Now move your asses."

Dak pulled Bless' shoulder, and the three of them sprinted across the sky bridge after Sid.

Bless made it to the end, just inside the adjacent building.

"Fire full auto spray," Hector yelled. He wanted to look back, but he knew he had to keep going. Hector was gone.

Together, he and others burst into the first stairwell they found and hustled down.

Sid was already on the ground level, waiting, tail wagging.

"Where to now, boss?" Tella kept the weapon in the ready position.

Julian pushed his commlink. "Citizen, do you copy?"

"I'm here."

"We need to know where the next closest com tower is."

Dak took a knee to watch the back door of the lobby they now stood in. No other troops could be seen directly outside.

"It won't take them long to figure out where we went." Tella kept scanning the ground outside

"Unless Hector stopped them." Dak glanced up with a hopeful expression.

Footsteps pounded on the staircase above them.

Dak's dash of hope dissolved, and he moved into position to begin shooting up at whatever entered the blast range.

"About twenty-five blocks to the north, you'll find the next com tower." Citizen's voice competed with the static on the line.

Damn. That would take forever.

There was no way he and the others could make it that far now. More explosions rocked the ground beneath him.

Dak, now kneeling, fired up the staircase.

Sid and Bless ran to the door and out into the street. Tella was right behind them. Bless stopped once he reached the next corner. More rifle fire sounded.

Dak came running after them. "Let's go."

He turned to run, and Tella screamed, the sound deafening. Bless looked back, and she was still rolling across the pavement. Blood streamed out of her back.

Dak turned to fire at a target, but there was none —at least, not that Bless could see.

Then she landed in a blur. The Syth-L assassin stood less than six feet away from Bless.

Sid jumped at her, and she caught the bot in the air and threw him into the street.

"Get out of the way." Dak swung his weapon around, and Bless dropped to the ground.

Within seconds, Dak opened fire at the Sythy, but she dove out of the way and rolled faster than Dak's rounds could track her. She somersaulted up and kicked Dak in the chest.

The big man flew backward. Bless drew his sword and attacked.

She ducked, bobbed, and side-stepped. Then kicked his hand. He lost his grip, and the sword skittered away.

Bless stepped back, arms raised.

She pulled a pulse pistol out of a thigh holster and leveled it at Bless.

Blam. The weapon went off.

A roar blew through Bless' ears, and a massive metal drone smashed the Sythy from the side, and Bless fell back.

The drone crashed onto the street with a shower of sparks and shredded asphalt.

Still prone on the ground, Bless shook his head, but the ringing in his ears continued.

The assassin staggered to her feet. Her head was caved in on one side, and one arm dangled freely. She had lost her pistol but Bless had seen where the weapon had landed.

He locked eyes with her, and she limped toward him.

Citizen flew out of nowhere and tackled her from the side. The two Sythys rolled and wrestled. Citizen let loose a flurry of punches and then blocked a counterattack. They tripped each other but held on.

Bless picked up his sword.

The assassin punched Citizen in the face, and her head snapped back. Pulling back again for another punch, the dark-headed Sythy grinned.

Sid's metal jaws clamped down on her good arm from behind, pulling her to the ground, and she yelled in pain or anger. He wasn't sure which it was.

She kicked Citizen in the face again. Citizen flew off. The Sythy got to her feet, but Sid dragged her around.

Dak charged, tackled her around the waist, and all three went down in a pile.

Sid's metal jaws had stripped almost all the flesh off her arm. Carbon fiber cables roped across the bones of her forearm.

Citizen landed on top of her and drove a dagger into her chest.

"Clear a path." Bless ran in and pulled back for a cut.

The assassin kicked Dak away and shrugged off Citizen.

Sid saw Bless and let go. His jaws chomped together, grinding steel on steel.

The assassin stepped back just in time to see Bless' blade whoosh down. His katana sliced through her neck, and her head popped off.

Bless landed in a crouch, ready for a backswing. But there was no need. The headless body swayed then fell back.

Sid jumped on the head and began attacking it, swinging it side to side by the hair, then tossed it down the street.

"That was close." Blood trickled down from a cut on Dak's forehead. "You okay?"

"Yeah, you?" Bless wiped the blade of his sword on the Syth-L assassin's torso.

"I'm good." A low-spirited expression covered Dak's face. "Tella's gone."

"Citizen?" Bless spun around, heart pounding in his chest. "Citiz—"

Citizen Hill was slowly getting up from one knee. Blood on her face and shirt cut in multiple places. She had so much blood on her. It couldn't be all hers.

"I'm okay." Citizen reached down and picked up the pulse pistol and stuck it in her waistband. She put her foot on the lifeless body and pulled out her dagger.

Dak picked up Tella's pulse rifle and handed it to Bless. "Now, let's get you to that next com tower."

"It's too far away." Bless held his head low, defeat only another pulse blast away.

"Not with this, Snowball." Citizen limped towards the transport drone. "Anyone up for a ride?"

23

CITIZEN HILL

'It should be on your right' Sunflower's text message flashed before her eyes.

"Why are we going to this one?" Dak peeked out a small window. "You said the other one was closer?"

"This is the one we're supposed to be at." Citizen eased the drone down.

It landed with a clang of metal on asphalt, jolting to a stop.

Dak jumped out first, rifle up. Sid was right behind him.

Citizen limped out behind them. Dak was already in the door to the com tower lobby.

'Power damper 4:18%,' displayed in blinking red

letters. An electrical surge buzzed the length of her body. She winced, then stumbled.

"You okay?" Bless took hold of her shoulder, nearly falling himself.

"No, but I'll be fine for a little while. Just get to the coms." She burst through the entry, shoving the door hard enough. It swung off its broken hinges.

Dak already had the elevator standing by. He had shot two security guards to clear their path—their bleeding bodies littered the hallway.

"There will be more upstairs." Bless pointed to the stairwell

Sid made a growl noise that sounded more like grinding gears, then ran up the staircase.

Citizen joined the rest of the group and Bless in the elevator.

She pulled out her pulse pistol. Dak and Bless pointed their rifles at the door.

The elevator dinged, and the group ran out, armed and ready. Only to find Sid was just finishing off the last of the guards who stood in front of the door.

'Use code 33407' Sunflower sent.

Citizen gave the code to Bless. He punched it in and went to the nearest console.

"Do you have to start all over?" Dak moved to the window.

"No, I saved it as a ghost file on the network. They won't find it for another twenty-four hours." His fingertips flew across the screen. "I've picked it back up. Just a few more walls to break. Hey, can you help me with this one?"

"What do you need me to do?" Citizen limped over and sat next to him.

"Find me the first ZPG file in this list." He pointed at one window. Her optics locked on and began a visual search.

"Here." She pointed.

"Damn, that was fast." He clicked it and kept opening windows.

'Tell him to use code GV67d63hE when he hits the wall,' Sunflower said.

"Here's the wall. It's asking for a security code." He sat as still as a stone statue, his hands poised over the screen.

Citizen relayed the code.

"Got it." His hands and fingers resumed their work. "We're inside."

"Thank you," whispered Citizen.

'No problem. Happy to help.'

"How long do we have until they discover our position?" Citizen asked the unknown Sunflower.

'Nearest troops are eleven minutes away. All drones

now search for you and your party, and those are five minutes away.'

'Power Damper 4: 13%' blinked in red.

"Activate emergency power." Her side ached. *'Emergency power supply 0%'* scrolled past her optics. "How much longer do you need, Bless?" Her vision darkened at the edges, then began to go blurry.

"Just a couple more minutes."

24

COMMANDER KARR

"There it is." Commander Karr pointed at the wind-shield. The com tower stood in front of them. "That's where they are."

"Location is already sent to Squads two, six, seven, and 10." The pilot readied the guidance system.

"Pull us up to floor five." Karr rubbed his hands together. "Zoom the camera all the way in." He had waited long enough for this day, and now, he wanted to relish every moment. "I want to see Bless die."

"Copy that, Sir." The pilot moved the giant drone.

"Squad two and six are already in position, Sir."

The co-pilot engineer paused. His index finger loomed over the enter key. "On your mark, Sir."

Finally, Bless would be out of his hair. He didn't know what had happened to the Syth-L assassin—didn't really care. He hadn't heard a report from Handler Meechum for quite a while either. But there was a major battle going on. She must've taken care of CH012SYTH-L, or he'd have heard from her by now.

I'll contact Meechum soon. He needed to inform her of a private part of the mission. He wanted the Sythy's circuit chip. But first, Bless needed to die. Dr. Drayson would be pleased, finally.

The missile drones floated into position.

"The two missile drones are ready, Sir." The co-pilot's eyes rested on him, awaiting command.

"Squads seven and ten are in a backup position." The pilot adjusted the microphone in front of his mouth. "Everyone is ready to breach, Sir."

"Excellent." Karr grinned and stood with his hands clasped behind his back. The camera zoomed in to get a better view of the fifth-floor windows. "Fire."

25

CITIZEN HILL

Pain jolted Citizen to an alert state.

Her vision grew more and more blurry. She was drained and knew it. She'd gotten them this far and now found herself struggling to remain operational.

Dak and Sid stood ready to defend the attackers.

"Here we go." Bless hit the enter key. "Thanks to you and your anonymous handler, we're in." Bless sat back. He breathed out and ran his hands through his messy hair. Then wiped away the dried blood from his cheek.

"And this will be recorded on the net?" Citizen leaned back in the chair, slouching.

"Yes, it will be broadcast live on every stream and

tower. But the recorded version will be available on the net. The Feds won't be able to kill the stream for at least four minutes." A smile bloomed on his face. "But the recorded version will take them a couple of days to erase."

"Whenever you're ready." Citizen clasped her right knee to keep it from moving during a spasm.

Bless cleared his throat and positioned himself in front of the camera, then pointed at Citizen. "Live in three, two, one."

Citizen hit the record button.

At that moment, Julian Bless changed his persona from rebel leader, guerrilla fighter, and chance-hacker into a statesman.

"Fellow residents of New Therian, my name is Doctor Julian Bless. Everything I have to say in the next four minutes makes me an enemy of the state. I have risked my life to bring you this information. I. Am. Elysium. I am the leader of a liberated group that has existed on the outside for years. We are a free people and do not fall under New Federation jurisdiction."

Rotating feed behind him depicted the atrocities of World War III and the birth of the New Federation, rising out of the ashes of the old, obliterated civilization of man.

"The New Federation Leadership once employed

me. I was the youngest member of The Microbiology Task Force that you have likely heard rumors about back then. Or Project Goldfish, as it was known to us. Project Goldfish was a secret genetic research program to enhance human DNA. This was never a benevolent program—still isn't today—it's a program meant to easier enslave Residents of the World Order under the leadership of the New Federation."

Genetic reports, schematics, and rolling clips of live experiments roll behind him on the monitors.

"I was primarily responsible for creating the RNA building blocks. But there was a problem, a grave one, and the biological coding mutated into a virus. And the virus created what we refer to as the Gollums and eventually the Scabbies or anyone who gets bitten by the Gollums. The virus escaped, infecting the entire countryside. The New Federation, primarily Dr. Drayson, covered up this incident and instead told everyone the virus was a random mutation in nature. They shut the program down, then place my family and me on watch." He pauses a moment, his voice wavering. "I alone escaped."

The monitors depict his detainment and that of his family and other scientists. Systematically, the screens show the death of those captured: car explosions, building fires, freak accidents, medical mysteries, suspicious suicides, and executions.

"About one year ago, the New Federation tried to undo this tragic mishap by spearheading another genetic initiative—experimentation on the Gollums. The experiments failed and created a bigger threat. A larger, smarter, and fiercer version that we then called Gollum 2.0s. This is why the protective dome was activated almost two weeks ago."

All images fade on-screen, replaced by a live drone feed of the attack on the city.

"A herd of these new Gollums attacked New Therian earlier today in sector eight. Right before the start of this broadcast. You likely heard about a firefight between rebels and New Federation patrols. This isn't true." He stills and pauses diplomatically. "I repeat, that information is false. Wreckage and bodies of these Gollum 2.0s can be seen and found with your own eyes in Sector 8 before the Fed shuts down access. Go there and see the truth for yourself."

Citizen looked out the window. Bless' image was broadcast on the outdoor flatscreens and billboards across the street. People stood, their necks craned up, listening in awe. This message was streamed on every channel, tower, device, screen, and audio output inside New Therian.

"The New Federation Leadership has lied to you for years. Dr. Drayson and his unofficial, unsanctioned, and illegitimate government is an enemy of all Residents. They have been hiding the truth. Once I stop this message, the New Federation Leadership or its troops will overwhelm you with propaganda to try and cloud that truth. I know some of you listening do not believe me. But I also know, some of you do—so, seek out the truth for yourselves."

More and more people swarmed the street, watching the broadcast. Citizen tried to zoom in closer to record the moment for prosperity, but the function remained unavailable due to her damaged state.

"Others of you don't know what you believe." Bless addressed the people direct as if to appeal to their humanity. "But you have a feeling in your heart, something more is out there. You have had this feeling long before you heard me. Deep down, you know there's something else; some truth you're missing. I encourage you to follow that feeling and see where it leads. Ask questions. Seek answers. Be skeptical of the New Federation and what they tell you. For whoever controls the information controls the people. So, today, I urge you to find the truth in your hearts as I did."

Bless drew in a deep breath, his facial expression softening.

"I will help you on your journey. Our strength is in our numbers. Together we are unstoppable. You may feel alone, but know you are not. The New Federation doesn't have enough power to over- whelm the strength of free and informed people. But you must continue the journey to freedom. The next step is to overthrow the New Federation together. This will be a long battle. I have come this far, but now I need your help to spread the word."

He gleamed straight into the camera lens, giving the people of New Therian a glimpse at the face of freedom—of Elysium.

"You can always find me. I am your path to freedom and the truth if you seek the truth. If you desire freedom, just ask for Elysium." He paused a moment. "Join me. Join Elysium. Be Elysium, for I am Elysium. All you have to do is ask for my name. But be careful when you do. The agents of the New Federation are everywhere, and they are watching. Believe in the truth, believe in freedom. I am Julian Bless. And I am Elysium." Bless nodded his head, and that was Citizen's cue to kill the feed.

Outside, a unified chant rose among the crowded viewers, "I. Am. Elysium."

26

JULIAN BLESS

"I am Julian Bless. I am Elysium." The video of Bless' face blinked off the screen inside Karr's drone. A New Federation logo went up on the screen.

"What the bloody hell was that?" Karr tossed a handheld device against the hull of the aircraft.

"I uh, I don't know, Sir." The co-pilot hit buttons on his control panel. "I don't know where the feed came from, I uh . . ."

"Why did we lose the audio from squad six? Where are they? I can see the drones firing into that com tower right in front of me. So, where the hell is my audio?"

"Audio feed is back up, Sir. Team 6, Sergeant Rios, is asking for you."

"Team six to Commander Karr." Sergeant Rios' image popped up on the screen.

"I'm here." The commander's teeth ground. "Where are they?"

"We are on the fifth floor now, Sir." His report squawked over the feed. "The drones fired, and I'm afraid no one is here."

"What do you mean, no one is there?" The vein on the side of Karr's head throbbed, matching the pounding headache taking him siege.

"There are no rebels, no bodies. The floor is empty, Sir." The feed flickered then cleared up. "They must have sent us to the wrong com tower?"

"That's impossible. The handler sent me these coordinates, and she ..."

No, it's not possible.

Karr felt his face go white, and his throat turned dry. Fear gripped his stomach, and he tried to swallow.

"Commander Karr." The co-pilot addressed him. "Dr. Drayson himself is requesting you on the secure line."

CITIZEN HILL

Citizen limped after Bless. Dak led the way. Their combined footsteps, and the buzzing of Sid's gears, echoed off the concrete basement walls.

'Power damper 4: 9%' flickered into view.

"We are directly under Building 44R now. The informant told me to go through this door." Citizen pointed up ahead.

"How low is your power?" Bless tied to support her under her arm.

"My fourth cell has an output of only nine percent. I have three other cells. But once this one goes down, I will lose a lot of motor function. I need a 'tinker' as soon as possible to repair the damper."

"And you think we're in the clear?" He held her gaze.

"Sunflower sent the troops to the other tower. Then she scrambled the drone footage from the others. It will take them quite a while to find out which tower we used. And by then, we'll be long gone."

"How do you know this Sunflower is a female?" Bless' brows shot up.

Citizen considered this. "I don't know. I just think so. It would be like what you call, a feeling, maybe?"

"This is the door." Dak held the handle. "Do I open it?"

Citizen looked at Bless, and he shrugged. She glanced at Sid.

The canine bot tilted his head, and his gears whined.

They've come this far—no need to stop now.

"Sunflower said she would be on the other side. We've got no other choice. Open it."

Dak pulled down on the latch to activate the exit mechanism. The door hinged open. Bless, and Dak held up their rifles.

"CH012?" A feminine voice flooded the hall.

"Yes. It is me."

A young blonde woman stepped out. Her hair was in a ponytail, and she wore the gray Federation uniform of a handler. Her face was quiet and peaceful. She smiled.

Citizen knew the smile meant something, so she tried to compute what.

"I'm Sunflower." The woman held out a hand.

Bless, and Dak lowered their rifles.

"My name is Nev Meechum. Nice to meet you." Her arm remained extended.

"Citizen Hill." She shook the young woman's hand. "Nice to meet you." A quick sidestep revealed the people behind her. "This is Julian Bless, Dak, and this charming bot is Sid."

Nev Meechum smiled at each one of them and left her gaze on Bless. "I am Elysium."

"I am Elysium." Bless met her declaration with affirmation and pride.

"We—I—just watched your message. It filled us all with hope. People are rioting in the streets. Troops are already trying to keep people away from seeing the bodies in sector eight. You, Dr. Bless, may have started a real revolution."

"I've waited a long time to do this." Nev Meechum walked up and embraced Citizen.

She hugged the young woman back. Even though

she knew of this gesture, she still didn't understand it completely.

"Come with me." Meechum motioned for her to follow. "I have two friends with me. One is a hacker and the other a tinker. They can repair you."

Meechum led her and Bless down another hallway and through two more doors. "We are in the bowels of Building 44R. This is part of the basement of the original structure before the new buildings were built. They have not found us here for weeks. We're safe, for now." She opened one more door.

Two men stood next to an old wooden table. A computer and a transfer station sat on a wheeled cart next to them.

"Dr. Bless." The first of the two men rose. "I. Am. Elysium. My name is Jerick."

The other person stepped forward. "I am Elysium. And my name is Athan. I am a tinker." He motioned to the table. "Citizen lay down. We can help you."

Citizen gingerly walked to the table and sat on the edge. She had expended most of her power and was so tired.

Bless, and Meechum helped her lay back.

Her gaze came to rest on Bless, her original target. He was alive, and that's all that mattered. And now, the town of Benton was safe. Most of the Troll herd was gone.

Bless had gotten his message out. And she was still alive, despite her run-in with a Syth-L assassin.

"Are you leaving, Snowball?"

"No, I'm staying right here." Under Bless' watchful eye, she allowed herself to relax.

Athan put on a pair of rubber gloves and began examining the wounds on her body. Jerick helped and began to remove the bandaging covering the older injury on her forearm.

"Just relax." Bless laced his fingers with hers. "They know what they're doing."

A needle pokes her shoulder, and her pain receptors adjusted. It must have been some kind of lidocaine. The tinker plugged the auxiliary port from her forearm into a jack.

A full-body diagnosis began. Something cut into her side, and both Athan and Jerick pushed their fingers in to find the damaged damper. More flesh was cut away. She turned her attention to the blonde young woman.

"Thank you for your help, Nev," Citizen's vision wavered, then cleared a bit.

"No. Thank you. For everything you did." Meechum walked closer.

"Tell me something." A spasm made her body tremble. "How did you find us?"

Nev smiled. "This truth that Dr. Bless talked about. I have felt it for a long time. But I never really knew what it was. Then by luck or fate, I was assigned to you. I was the original handler for Operation 219. So, I've been with you for a while."

"Yes, you seemed familiar. Not just your voice, but your face also."

"I reported directly to Commander Karr himself. And one day, I returned to my terminal and found someone had logged on while I was gone, but I didn't know the new 7.0 update required a code to log out properly. It must have been someone who wasn't using the net all day like we do. So, I backtracked and found out it was Commander Karr who had used my terminal."

"Why?" Bless adjusted his hold on Citizen's hand and stroked her thumb and wrist—a human comforting gesture, one she was aware of.

"Yeah, I wondered why, too, so I began tracking his activity. That's when I discovered he had ties to Operation Blue Thunder. And what I found in those files confirmed some of my suspicions—some of my feelings. I started to do more research. I knew the Federation wasn't right. And from what I had learned from Bless' files and the info we had on Elysium. I slowly saw the light." She nodded to Bless.

Bless returned the gesture with a twinkle in his eye. "You're welcome."

"When Commander Karr put my entire family and me under surveillance, I began relaying info via text to help you."

"That was dangerous." Bless held her gaze. "And very brave."

"It was a great deal of help." A surge of electricity slammed through Citizen from what Athan was doing. "We couldn't have done it without you."

"You deserve to know more." Nev let out a long sigh. "In those files, I found truth not only for me but for you too, Citizen."

"What do you mean?" A sharp pain stabbed at her side, and she did her best to ride the wave of pain without losing consciousness.

"All in good time." Nev patted Citizen's shoulder. "First thing first, let's get you fixed up for now."

"But why did you do all of this?" Citizen blinked back the darkness threatening to suck her into an abyss of nothingness.

"I just had to. I had no choice." Meechum smiled. "Now, rest."

A philosophical quote popped up on her display,

and she read it out loud. "I cannot teach anybody anything. I can only make them think."

The wording perplexed her. *Why these words, why now?*

"The new damper is in place." Athan wiped his hands off. "It will take some time to charge the cell. Do you want to install the chip?"

"What chip?" Citizen turned her gaze on him.

"Send it." Nev nodded to Athan. "I retrieved this for you, Citizen."

'Emotion Package XY BETA,' displayed in her vision input. *'Install YES or NO.'*

The latest emotion chip. The most advanced emotion package any Syth-L can acquire and run.

This chip would allow her to bypass her programming and prevent her from turning Bless in, finally. It was what she had been after—what she needed. This would help her along her journey—to understand humans better.

This will enable me to feel, help me to become more, well, human.

She couldn't tell if this was the right decision or not. She then recalled Julian's speech from a little while ago and repeated the words out loud.

"I have come this far by myself. But now I need your help. I want you to know you can always find me. I am your path to freedom and the truth." She paused a moment, then added something of her own. "For those who want to know more and desire to seek out the truth—the one truth now knocking at your soul. You can always find me. I. Am. Elysium."

She focused, then selected 'YES,' and the emotion chip began installing inside her.

THE END

SNEAK PEEK: NEW THERIAN CITY

CITIZEN HILL: BOOK 2

Hell knows no fury like a scorched and scorned Syth-L.

With his message now out, Bless fans the flames of a revolution, seeking to free the people from the federation's stronghold. He'll stop at nothing to atone for the wrongs of his past and of those still in power.

Citizen yearns to become as human as possible and discovers more about her parents. Still "enemies" on paper, Bless a rebel and Citizen a Fed agent, must find some common ground to stand on without cracking in the process.

Her call to duty and his need to rectify grave wrongs lends them on an unknown path full of conflict and destruction.

1

CITIZEN HILL

'Diagnostic complete' read across Citizen's GUI vision. 'Neuro-receptors 92%.' Citizen stood and rotated her head on her neck, stretching her stiff muscles. It had been two full days since they had survived the battle in the city, thanks to Nev Meechum.

"How are you feeling?" Nev walked up and held out a bottle of water.

"Just fine." Citizen grabbed the bottle and took a long drink. "Any news from up top?"

"The riots are still going. The Feds don't know what to do. A lot of people have been talking about

Elysium. We expect the numbers to grow in the underground."

"That's good news."

"The lines are saying the Federation Troops have finally quit staffing Sector 8 and have pulled back, creating a perimeter. Most of the civilians are out now."

"So, the Trolls are still attacking?"

"Yes, they apparently offered a bigger fight than the troops had anticipated."

"Yeah, they are a lot smarter than the old ones." Citizen finished the water bottle.

"And we've captured a working drone finally. Athan has it up in the garage. We want Julian to take a look at it when he can. If he can break the code on it, that would be a great help."

"I can do that." Julian Bless walked into the room. "How is that new emotion chip treating you?" Bless sat on the bench and took out his cleaning kit, unfolded the oily cloth, and then began wiping the blade of his katana. The Damascus steel gleamed under the light.

Citizen's adaptive programs of her learning CPU had fully internalized the XY Beta Chip, but she still didn't know exactly how they worked. "The emotions are available for me to draw upon.

However, it seems like I can't pull them up like any other program."

Bless nodded. "Yes, probably because that's how emotions work."

"What do you mean?"

"I mean, for all of us, the emotions are there." He set the oily cloth down and picked up the dry stopper. "But rarely are emotions something we bring up initially. We usually respond to a certain stimulus with the emotion."

She was still learning how to fully understand these human feelings. Whatever she knew of human thinking before was extraordinarily little compared to her level of exposure now. It was amazing how just access to these new emotions made her process things differently. "But how do you know which emotion to choose in your response?"

Bless smiled, his eyes never leaving his blade. "That's the point. You don't select an emotion like you would choose a combat program. You just respond naturally. You allow the emotion to express itself." Once the dry stopper had covered the blade in its appropriate places, be put the bottle down and began massaging the oil into the blade with the cloth.

"So, I do not have control over my emotions?"

This thought did little for her. The notation of having no control over one's self didn't compute.

"No, no. That's not entirely accurate. In a sense, yes, you don't have much control when a certain emotion comes out. You do, however, have control over how you choose to react to said emotion."

The words he was saying made sense, but she still needed more context. He looked at her and must have been able to read it in her face.

"For instance." He finished with the cloth and began packing away the cleaning kit. "Let's say you walk around the corner, and someone punches you in the face."

"Okay." Kind of a strange example, but fine.

"Now, what emotion would you likely feel when that happened?"

"Surprise or anger, I suppose."

Not to mention, a fight mode simulation would acti-vate, initiating combat mode.

"Good, yes. That would work. Maybe even contempt or fear. In fact, you may have a rush of all four of those different emotions."

"So, you can have more than one emotion at a time?"

"Of course." Bless held his sword in front of him and looked up and down its spine. "That is fairly common, actually." Satisfied with his work, he began to re-sheath the sword. "For simplicity, let's say it is just anger that comes out. No one is there to hurt you or kill you. They are just trying to get your attention."

"That does not seem like a very successful method of getting my attention."

"You're right. But just for the sake of the point, I'm trying to make, let's say you feel anger."

"Okay."

"Now that you feel the emotion, you can decide to react to it or respond to it." He looked into her eyes as he sat down.

"React or respond?"

"Yep. That's what I said."

Those two phrases had similar, almost interchange definitions, but there was some other point Bless was trying to make with these words. But that point remained in the shadows of her processing unit.

"What is the difference?"

"Re-acting is when you don't think, and you simply respond to the anger and punch the person in the face. Responding is when you think about it, realize that no violence is needed, and you choose to not respond in anger but to do something else instead."

"So, you're saying when I have an emotion. I can still choose how I respond to that emotion?"

"Correct."

"So, responding is always better than reacting?"

"Not necessarily. Many times, yes, but sometimes, you won't have time to think about it, especially in combat. Or there might be times when reacting naturally is perfectly fine. Reacting isn't necessarily bad. It's simply good to know the difference between the two."

She scrunched her eyebrows. "So, how do I know when to react or respond?"

Bless leaned in and pointed his finger at her. "That is one of the hardest things to figure out. There is no clear-cut answer all the time. Sometimes we have to, well, feel instead of just think. And that is one of the things that makes us human. It is a substantial portion of our humanity."

Another layer of humanity. This was all so strange. It seemed like as soon as she learned one thing, two more concepts popped up. It was like she was unwrapping a ball made of nano-cord. No matter how many strands she pulled apart, it would separate into two more strings.

Will the process of understanding humans be never-ending? It was confusing enough to make the circuits in her brain whirl.

"It is puzzling still, isn't it?"

Citizen nodded. "Yes. But it is not something that discourages me from learning more about you. I understand it. I just think I need more experience—more data input to analyze."

Bless chuckled. The sound annoyed her, which, in the greater scheme of things, was yet another emotion she had not mastered.

"Are you guys ready?" Nev was standing in the doorway with her Federation jacket on.

"Yes." Bless got up, and Citizen followed.

"I have to report to the station in one hour." Nev led the way to the ladder.

"Dak, you ready?" Bless called to their massively large teammate.

"Yes, sir." Dak was twice the size of Bless and almost as strong as Citizen, or so it seemed.

Sid jumped to his paws, and his gears whirled and creaked as the bot walked. His metal claws clicked off the metal floor.

"I will leave you at the garage." Nev pulled her hair back into a ponytail and placed the gray Federation cap on. "I will have to be at the station until 1400 hours. We won't meet up back here. I will find where you are staying once I can check with Athan." She rested one hand on the ladder rung.

"Okay." Bless nodded. "We'll trust Athan and go where he tells us."

Nev turned and began ascending the ladder. Bless went next.

Citizen felt compelled to go immediately after him because even though they were in a safe house, she could not let anything happen to him. She looked down.

Dak grabbed Sid by the shoulder handle and lifted the bot with him, and then climbed the ladder with one hand.

2

JULIAN BLESS

"For the next two days, we'll stay in one of the underground transit tunnels." Nev led them down a hall. "We have learned that if the leadership remains in one physical location for over two days, we eventually get raided. So, we try to stay on the move."

"So, you do not have one central location for Elysium leadership to meet?" Citizen kept pace next to Bless.

"Not necessarily." Nev opened a door and looked both ways down a T intersection before continuing. "It is too dangerous to stay in one location for too long. The leadership of the network is loose but effective. It is the only way for the network to continue if someone's captured. And even if they're tortured by the Feds, they won't know enough about the networks as a whole to reveal enough information that could kill it completely."

"The challenge with this type of network is an alignment of goals." Julian adjusted his katana so the tip didn't bang on the stainless-steel doorframe.

"Yes," said Nev. "Exactly."

"I understand there is no other way to grow a movement like this underground. But my experience with Elysium on the outside, out in the autonomous zone, taught me that the number one enemy was not the Federation on the outside. Still, it was a miscommunication from within."

"A lesson learned the hard way, I imagine." Nev kept walking.

"With a loose network like this, there is always a high possibility that two different factions may end up with competing goals." Thoughts of Durham and the Elysium split still plagued his memory.

Nev looked over her shoulder at him and Citizen, then allowed them both to catch up.

"Yes, I understand. I am new to the movement myself," said Nev. "That's why we are all inspired by your presence here. You have learned lessons we need to know. We need to learn from you."

Bless stopped next to her. "I will try."

"There have been many people here in New Therian that heard about Elysium for a long time. But back then, it was only rumored. We wanted them to be true. We wanted to believe in Julian Bless."

Her words made him feel inadequate because he wasn't sure he could measure up to the myth and lore created in his name.

"Many of us were trying to find a way out of the city like you did." Nev glanced at him. "The bravery and courage you showed by actually coming to us, back into the city, made believers out of all of us."

"I can only do my best." Bless stretched his shoulders back. The stress of his newfound fame made his muscle knot. "Elysium is strong. But at its roots, it comprises of people—of humans from all walks of life, shapes, and sizes. And many with different views on matters of state, but they all agree on one thing."

"Which is?" Nev glanced his way again.

"That human beings have the capability to make choices, good or bad."

"And we've all seen the result of bad choices," said Nev. "Death and destruction often follow, which is why people need to ban together—build unity to take out the bad seed, the Federation."

"We recently had a terrible split of Elysium back

in the Autonomous Zone. Many of my followers chose to follow someone else. It was my greatest leadership failure. It bothers me to this day."

"Then we will guard against that here." Her words rung with confidence.

"We should keep moving." Citizen's head froze like her scanners were picking up drone codes.

The drones were above ground and would not detect them, but the presence of Federal Agents could be nearby.

"Let's talk once we get to the safe house." She was all business on the outside, but Bless wondered what was going on internally, at least, from an emotional stance.

It must be odd to experience feelings—something she'd never had to compute before.

"Of course." Nev began leading the group again. They quickly made their way through a few more twists and turns and into another tunnel that eventually opened to a large underground rail station.

Julian Bless followed Nev inside. And Citizen followed him along with Sid, and Dak kept the rear position.

The taller man had to duck considerably to get his massive body through the rounded door frame. Once inside, Dak closed the hatch.

Bless and the rest of the group now stood in the

abandoned rail station depot. From the dust on the tracks and the level of rust on much of the metal, it was clear it was no longer active.

Two older men stood opposite a table. A tall woman occupied the spot next to the only working computer monitor on the railway terminal. The computer was a portable, folding type, yet plugged into the railway circuit board.

"Everyone." Nev's voice echoed off the large, soundless room. "I'd like you to meet Julian Bless." She gestured to him. The three others in the room walked up. "And this is Citizen Hill, a Syth-L that is on our side."

Several murmurs whispered around the room, and the onlookers looked on in awe.

"This is Dak." Nev bent down. "And this here is Sid." She pointed to the bot.

Sid's gears whirled, and he sat on his haunches in perfect obedience.

"They have recently fought their way into the city, and they're here to help," said Nev.

"I am Elysium." Julian nodded to the three of them.

"I am Elysium." All three of them said in unison.

"This is Starkley." Nev pointed to the tall woman with long blonde hair. "Starkley has been with the network for months and has the most accurate knowledge of the sub rail system. She also obtained a Level 9 certification in binary cipher from the Federation Agency before joining us."

"Impressive." Julian smiled. "We are honored to have you as an associate."

"Likewise." Starkley offered a smile in response.

"This is Hanko." Nev pointed to the man with long gray hair who stood in the middle.

"An honor to meet you, Mr. Bless." Hanko had small eyes behind tiny round-lensed glasses.

His hair was a wild mess of gray tangles. And from the looks of things, no attempt to control it had occurred for some time. He wore a long gray coat that reached past his knees.

"Hanko was a street vendor before joining the network and is our chief counter-intelligence specialist. He has contacts in literally every sector of the city and has more methods of communication than the Federation itself."

"Thank you," said Bless. "I'm looking forward to working with you."

"And this is Tremmel." She introduced the last man.

Tremmel was much older than Bless. He stood ramrod straight with his hands behind his back like he was stepping up for a military inspection. Wrinkles and lines filled a grizzled face. He had one cheek covered in pockmarks—the other remained smooth. His face was motionless and rigid. But his eyes were even harder.

His flat top of gray hair and his stiff posture made him appear like a former soldier.

"Thank you, Julian Bless, for everything. We are glad you're here." Tremmel bowed his head. As he spoke, deep lines of crow's feet shot out from the corners of his eyes. "I was a Federation Soldier for fourteen years, a Sergeant in the Compliance Division."

No wonder. Bless had gotten good at noticing minuscule details about people. So much about a person could be gained from noticing the little details. Surviving by making gut decisions on people quickly had kept him alive.

"This is the core of the network leadership." Nev dropped her hands and turned back to Bless.

"But now you are here," Tremmel spoke first. "We are calling ourselves the Elysium Underground Network. Our numbers have almost doubled since your broadcast two days ago."

"That's good to know," said Bless.

"The news of the virus' origin—created by the Federation—has been a moment of enlightenment for many. Please." Tremmel motioned to the table.

Everyone moved to stand around it. On the metal

table lay an old paper map of New Therian. It contained coffee stains and frayed lines showing it had been folded and stored repeatedly for years.

"We know this is an old map and parts of it are not accurate," Starkley said. "But it is useful to keep since it keeps us from putting Elysium locations on any grid that can be hacked."

"So," said Bless. "Where are you on here?"

"This is us now." She pointed to Sector 21 in the corner. "The Feds are still fighting the Trolls and Gollums in the breach over here in Sector 8." She went on to tap a spot. "So, for the time being, most of their resources are tied up there."

"Good to know," said Bless.

"Yeah," replied Starkley. "But there are still plenty of eyes and cameras looking for Elysium."

"Do we know which garrisons they're deploying to fight in Sector 8?" Citizen stood next to Bless.

Tremmel took over. "So far, we believe that it's every garrison in Section 8 and all adjoining sections. APC Drones from all over the city have been moving to and from this area."

Citizen nodded. "I would like to get back to Sector 8 to damage their supply lines. If I could disrupt the drone programming, that could cause a lot of havoc. I will be back before the end of the day tomorrow."

Tremmel studied Citizen then pointed back down on the map. "From here to Sector 8, we have at least three safe houses that I know of. This would be the fastest route. However, the fastest route is usually not the safest."

"Understood."

"Should you get into trouble." Tremmel's face creased tighter, and he squinted at a square on the map. "This building here at 9.G2 is a cantina called Nagano's. The owner's named Kenji, and he's always behind the bar."

"Note taken." Citizen nodded.

"He is Elysium," said Tremmel. "He's a sympathizer to our cause, but his entire establishment is covert, so be careful what you say and to whom."

"Understood." Citizen traced the line from the current location to Sector 8 with the tip of her index finger.

"He can get you into Sector 8. Here is a picture of him." Tremmel pulled a data-pad out of his pocket and tapped the screen.

Citizen saw the man's face, and she nodded, probably recording the image in her vision.

"I will leave today," she said to no one in particular.

"Okay," said Bless. "Nev, you're going back to HQ, correct?"

"Yes, I have to be there in an hour, or they will get suspicious."

Bless pointed to Dak and Sid. "Dak, I want you to stay here and secure this space." He turned to Starkley, Hanko, and Tremmel. "I would like to meet our newest Elysium as soon as possible."

"Before we go"—Starkley held up her hand—"If we are assaulted, and we have to abandon this place, our second rally point is here." She pointed to the map. "It is a dilapidated apartment complex. Mostly junkies and squatters there. Our code word for the move to the second rally point is Gold."

"Gold." The word rolled off Citizen's lips.

"Gold, it is." Bless looked around. From Citizen and Dak, then to Nev and his three new allies. He was more enthusiastic than he could remember.

"I'll see you all tomorrow." Citizen took her leave.

ACKNOWLEDGMENTS

Special things go out to the people who encouraged me to write this body of work. Without you, this body would still live in the recess of my brain, searching for a way out.

Thank you. And you each know who you are!

ABOUT THE AUTHOR

Simon Sayz is a pen name for an American writer who lives in the US, traveling from one fictional place to another with pets Riley, a wolf spider living in the shadows, and Tibias, the dust bunny with a bad attitude, who, at this ungodly hour, lurks under the couch.

www.ingramcontent.com/pod-product-compliance
Lightning Source LLC
Chambersburg PA
CBHW071851220626
47052CB00002B/64